THE GHOST AND THE FORGER

I0671922

THE CHESHIRE PRESS

THE GHOST AND THE FORGER

THE GHOST
and the
FORGER

A Nell Bane Novel

Nancy Parsons

THE GHOST AND THE FORGER
Nancy Parsons

Published by
The Cheshire Press
A Division of The Cheshire Group, Inc.
PO Box 2090
Andover, MA 01810
www.cheshirepress.com

ISBN: 978-0-9995092-4-1
Library of Congress Control Number: 2017954226

Printed in the United States of America

This is a work of fiction. Any resemblance to individuals or
occupations are purely coincidental. All trademarks used herein are for
identification only and are used without intent to infringe on the
owner's trademarks or other property rights.

Cover design by Nancy Parsons

Parsons, Nancy
The Ghost and the Forger

THE GHOST AND THE FORGER

For Don Doyle

Also by Nancy Parsons

More From The Better Mousetrap
with Dick Amsterdam

Bald As A Bean: The Experience of Sudden Hair Loss

Abigail's Unicorn

Ye Canna Join In Oor Games
Memories of a Scottish-American Childhood

Brothers of War: The P.O.W. Experience
with James F. Arsenault

The Dog That Managed Hedge Funds

—The Nell Bane Novels —
Two-Thirds of a Ghost
The Ghost Works A Puzzle
The Ghost Ties A Double Knot
The Ghost Paints A Portrait
The Ghost Lays the Ghosts to Rest
The Ghost and the Forger

THE GHOST AND THE FORGER

Caveat emptor

THE GHOST AND THE FORGER

CHAPTER 1

If an actual elf had appeared on Nell Bane's doorstep, she couldn't have been more surprised.

"H.H. Willoughby, Mrs. Bane," the elf said, "My card."

Wonderingly, Nell accepted the elderly gentleman's crisp business card, which was delivered with an old-fashioned bow.

"What exquisite calligraphy!" she exclaimed. "H. H. Willoughby," she read. She looked up inquiringly.

"Henry Herbert," he elaborated genially. "Henry to those who best know me."

"Currency, documents, art antiquities," Nell continued reading. "What exactly does this mean?"

She raised her eyes in wonder to the old man's face and found his blue eyes crinkling at the corners and actually twinkling, the way Santa Claus's eyes are said to twinkle.

"Calligraphy," he said modestly, "is my profession. Or one of them. I work with pen and ink. Also, on occasion, with sable brushes and paints. But the card is a bit vague...intentionally so. My work is much like yours, Mrs. Bane. I simply do whatever my clients require. I am merely a conduit. A means to their ends."

This explanation deepened Nell's impression that this small fellow had other-worldly powers. They had never met—she was sure they hadn't—yet he seemed to know a great deal about her. Her name, for instance, how did he know her name? And he seemed to have knowledge of her ghostwriting occupation, but how?

She hastily gathered her scattered wits.

"Well, Mr. Willoughby, I guess you'd better come in so we can become better acquainted."

Now I'm sounding like him, Nell told herself as she led the elf down the narrow hall toward the sunny kitchen and snug at the back of the little house. That shouldn't have surprised her. Her skill as a ghostwriter required her to submerge her own voice into the client's and, like some benevolent dybbuk, to speak and write in her subject's voice.

"The kitchen," Nell explained, "is the heart of this house. Everyone and every activity gravitates toward it, so now that you are here too, you must tell me how you found your way here."

To herself, she added, Now stop it! Stop it right now!

Henry Willoughby seated himself on the sofa in the snug and squirmed back among the cushions pleasurably. Nell noticed his feet did not reach the floor.

"You are a ghostwriter, Mrs. Bane," he told her, "and on the recommendation of a great friend of mine, I am seeking you out to write a memoir. Perhaps you remember him? Angus Titus?"

"Angus!" Nell was delighted. "That wonderful man. I loved working on his stories of the sea. As we finished, Angus gave me the gift of that Aga," Nell pointed toward the cooker in the kitchen. "I love to make soup and the Aga is the perfect thing."

Henry Willoughby beamed as if he himself had presented Nell with the perfect thing for making soup. He seemed quite pleased with himself.

"I am retired now," he said. "Eighty-six years, yes, and it was time to retire. Oh, the hand is as steady as ever, but it seemed time to lay down brush and pen and enjoy some leisure. Seek other pastures. Hound after other pursuits. So, taking a leaf from Angus's book—pun unintentional, there, Mrs. Bane—I decided it was time to write my memoir, for there are amazing tales to be told."

Willoughby paused, apparently recalling some of the tales, and he shook his head appreciatively. Then he chuckled.

Nell waited. Patience was another tool of the ghostwriter. You had to be patient and let the client's stories leak out or spill out in whatever cadence required. In the interval, Nell studied her guest.

Tufts of thick white hair sprouted above each ear while north of these tufts, Henry's baldhead shone as if polished. The elaborate bowtie—navy blue with cream-colored polka-dots—had obviously been tied and perhaps re-tied, with loving attention, and a matching handkerchief spilled from a breast pocket. His shoes—what must they be? Size six?—shone as brightly as his scalp.

H.H. Willoughby resumed the narration.

"For sixty years my clients have come to me—heard of my reputation, they have—and I've done the work as they've asked. Some of that work, Mrs. Bane, has been fascinating and some has been dangerous. Some of the results have been uplifting, and some have been disastrous. But it is all grist for the mill. All grist for the memoir of H. H. Willoughby, master of the pen and brush."

At these last words, Nell's eyelids shot up like snapped window shades. Why hadn't she picked up on the clues

Willoughby had dropped? What, exactly, was his line of work?

"Mr. Willoughby," Nell began carefully, "if you had to describe your profession, what would you say?"

"Why, my dear, I thought you understood. I specialize in forgery. I am a forger."

CHAPTER 2

"He seemed proud of it, Robert," Nell marveled, relaying to her friend Robert Hutchins the details of her meeting with H.H. Willoughby. "He just came right out and admitted it, admitted he was a forger. It was on the tip of my tongue to ask if he'd ever been in jail."

"And?" Robert said encouragingly.

"I gather not," Nell answered.

Robert cleared his throat and looked thoughtful.

"And you are accepting this...er...this individual as a client?"

Nell nodded.

"Well, you'd better be sure his checks clear," Robert cautioned drily, "and if you accept any paper currency, you'd better trot right down to the bank and have it authenticated. I know you, Nell, you're too trusting, and taking on a client with this rather jaundiced *modus operandi* is risky, even for you."

Nell made a *pish-toshing* sound that caused Robert Hutchins to pinch his lips reproachfully and repeat his warning.

"What's a *modus operandi?*" Bunty Whitney wanted to know. Nell's backdoor neighbor was leaning on the kitchen counter with her chin in both hands. She was fascinated.

Looking professorial, Robert recited, "A *modus operandi,* or m.o., is a distinct pattern or method of operation indicating or suggesting the work of a single criminal operating in a series of crimes," he told her. Then, with a meaningful look at Nell, he added, "I can't think of a more fitting description of a forger than that."

Robert's partner, Jerry Gasso, on the other hand, was delighted.

"Nellybean! Super score! Delicious. Can't wait for all the details. And when do I get to meet the fellow? Get to shake the hand that has corrupted hundreds? Bilked thousands?"

"Jerry!" Nell was scandalized."

Jerry Gasso chuckled.

"Admit it, Nellybean, you turn up the most amazing characters as clients."

Bunty Whitney now felt free to put in her oar.

"You got that right, Jerry. Remember the guy who invented himself right into the midst of the 9/11 drama, thus saving the children of all those victims?"

"Ha!" Jerry exclaimed, adding, "or the babe who stalked the judge's daughter and hired a thug to tip the girl in front of the Orange Line train?"

"Or that demented little professor in Ipswich who was enthralled with the idea of the perfect woman and who tried to kill his wife by driving into a tree?"

Nell protested. "Come on, you two. None of that was as bad as you make it sound. And I am really quite keen on this project. I think it will be fascinating. I mean, how does one become a forger? Do you consciously decide to pursue it, the way you'd decide to study medicine or engineering? Or do you sort of fall into it through happenstance? Like, one day you take a wrong turn and then another and first thing you know, there you are up to your neck and forging away on all sorts of illicit documents?"

"Nell," said Bunty pragmatically, "you think too much. And by the way, your eyes have a peculiar gleam. This project might not be good for you, you know. You'd better be careful."

And so, warned by Bunty Whitney and by Robert Hutchins, who was nodding vigorously in support of Bunty, Nell felt obliged to redeem herself, and she privately vowed to go forward, hand-in-hand-with the elfin H.H. Willoughby, and to write the memoir of an honest-to-goodness forger.

CHAPTER 3

It was nearly a week before Nell could bring herself to deposit Henry Willoughby's check. She couldn't get over the elegant script that had turned a plain blue bank draft into a piece of art. But finally, mindful of Robert Hutchins's warning about depositing any check from Willoughby promptly in order to establish its veracity, Nell drove to the branch and waited duly in line.

"Oh my, this is beautiful, isn't it?" Hetty Varnum said as she punched in the amount. "Almost too pretty to cash."

Nell agreed. She'd propped the check on the mantel in the snug and had felt a small twinge when she finally had to release it into her bank account. She'd kept the envelope though, and had taken an odd pleasure in seeing her own name and address rendered so handsomely. The envelope was still on the mantel.

But business was business, and having settled on an estimate for the entire project, Nell had explained to Henry Willoughby that her standard compensation was one-third, one-third-and one-third: the first installment due at the start of the project, the second at mid-point, and the final third when Nell turned in the finished manuscript of the memoir.

Henry Willoughby had been keen to understand the workings and underpinnings of the ghostwriting business, and Nell had explained that they would meet regularly so Henry could relate the day's memoir session.

"You can select whatever you want to talk about," Nell told him. "It doesn't have to be chronological or in any order at all. After we've been underway for a while, the memoir will begin to take its own shape. I'll be able to see its shape when it ripens and then, can cut and paste and work up the form."

"So I am free to choose any topics I wish?" Henry had asked, seeking confirmation.

And with assurances that he could, Nell had gone on to explain how she would record the sessions with her tiny Sony recorder so she could listen again and again as she wrote up a draft of each session.

"I'd like to work where you are comfortable," she had said. "I will want to absorb your environment and try to feel what you feel. As well, I will learn, by listening to you and to the recordings, to think as you do. Your speech patterns and mannerisms will become mine. Most people have little sayings and clichés that they use often, and I'll pick up on these and begin to use them too. For a while, Henry—for as long as we work together on this project—your voice will be in my mind. It will become my voice in some measure. It's a rather odd experience, but usually I find it pleasurable."

All of this seemed agreeable to Henry Willoughby, and good as his word, his personal check arrived in Nell's mailbox several days later.

She made a mental note to ask him about the calligraphy on the check. She had always been slightly vain about her own handwriting—a plain, but clear, Palmer method cursive learned in third grade that was distinctive only in its evenness and readability. A sensible, legible script produced with a five dollar gel pen that refused to leak or blot or skip. She tried to imagine herself producing a product like Willoughby's and could only shake her head in wonder.

"Ah, the distinction between a professional and a semi-talented amateur," she sighed. "Best stick to the profession I know best."

CHAPTER 4

"Welcome to the family manse," Henry Willoughby said by way of greeting. "I trust you found your way without difficulty?"

"No trouble at all," Nell told him. "Just cruised down Route 1 about three miles from my house in Newburyport, and now—here I am."

Willoughby's house, she noted, was more elderly than the old gentleman himself, and it was so full of antiquities and objects that its owner was forced to negotiate the house on tight paths. These paths were clear, though, marked by worn rivers in the ancient carpets where warp and woof showed the way. Cups and plates cluttered every surface, framed documents and paintings hung on walls and leaned against other objects.

"My *lares* and *penates*," Henry explained cheerfully, gesturing.

"Ah," Nell nodded, looking around "So I see—the cherished deities of home and hearth."

"Quite so. I'm the sixth generation of Willoughbys to

occupy the premises."

He paused, to look around. "Six generations worth of chattel," he observed mildly. "But," he added as he resumed walking, "you'll be most interested in The Shop. Step this way."

"Some would call this a studio," Nell observed when she had been led to the small room at the far end of the house that had once, perhaps, been a keeping room. "But you say shop?"

"Yes. Nothing so grand as a studio. Just a nook where the work gets done."

An enormous drawing board took up most of The Shop's space. Pots of ink, wrenched-looking tubes of paint and paint-blotched palettes surrounded the board, and brushes and pens bloomed from jugs like robotic blossoms. Like a giant bird from a science fiction film, a hinged gooseneck lamp loomed—or lurked—over the drawing board.

"Color-corrected bulb," Henry said, indicating the lamp.

"I am more comfortable here than any place else on earth," he declared. "Do you think this would be a good place for you to work as well?"

Nell looked around, hoping she didn't look as dubious as she felt.

"If it is where you are comfortable," she said bravely, "and if you can find me a comfortable chair and a bit of light, I can work in The Shop perfectly well."

Looking relieved, Henry Willoughby scurried around and produced an ancient armchair upholstered in a prickly fabric. Next he dragged a brass floor lamp from a dark corner, plugged it in, and a circle of yellow light that somehow seemed as elderly as everything else in the room, vaguely illuminated the chair. Nell was able to see that the fabric had a pattern. Roses.

"This will be just fine," she declared. "Shall we begin?"

Ever since her conversation with her friends in the kitchen, Nell had been keen to know how one got into the forgery game, and now she was able to ask Henry Willoughby directly.

Willoughby ran a hand over his mouth and gazed toward the ceiling of The Shop.

"Let's see..." he said.

Nell had the impression that his memory was reeling backward through time and would stop when it got to the file marked "beginning."

"Ah."

She saw that it had stopped. He was there.

"It was back when I was an art student studying at the Museum School, so it would have been..." his tongue clicked on the roof of his mouth. "... let's see...I was born in 1930 just before...*click-click*... of course. And I'll tell you in a minute why I remember that date.

"I was living at the time in student quarters, you see— living in genteel penury—when Forsyth the Younger invited himself into my digs with a proposition. Forsyth the Younger wanted me to create identification that would indicate he was of legal age to get a drink at any establishment in Boston.

"Forsyth the Elder, you see, was a big mucky-muck on Beacon Hill, and his son did pretty much what he wanted and got away with most of it. Well, in 1933, prohibition had just ended and Boston lawmakers, among them Forsyth the Elder, I presume, thought it proper to establish a legal drinking age, and they settled on twenty-one. Why? Well, you may well ask why. Because twenty-one had already been established as the legal voting age. So they didn't have to be too creative, up there on Beacon Hill. They didn't have to think very hard. On Beacon Hill, thinking is often discouraged.

"So I did as Forsyth the Younger requested, and he paid me rather handsomely, I thought. And then Forsyth the Younger sent over a number of other young Harvard men, all requiring my services, and he had, I may tell you, an astonishing number of friends and acquaintances all of whom had connections, and for a while I was almost too busy to attend my painting classes over at the Museum School.

"So that was how it began, I suppose, but I will tell you this."

And Henry Willoughby wagged a serious forefinger at Nell to be sure he had her attention—sure she would mark and remember his words.

"No person who carried an H.H. Willoughby I.D. was ever arrested for violating the legal drinking age."

He paused, and the elfin smile danced at the corners of his mouth.

"That is not to say, my dear, that no one was never *arrested*. Goodness no. For public drunkenness, yes, they got arrested right and left, but never—never— for carrying improper credentials."

CHAPTER 5

"Now that I've accepted an admitted forger as a client," Nell told Robert Hutchins, "I'm discovering there's a lot to learn about his subject."

Robert wasn't entirely sympathetic, but he was patient. He was also accustomed to serving as a sounding board when Nell was puzzling out the details of her clients' situations. And on this particular day, the sounding board was treating Nell to lunch at Brine on Newburyport's State Street.

"What have you learned so far?"

"There are various types of forgery, Robert, were you aware of that?"

"Indeed?" Robert feigned surprise, but he smiled as he did so and said encouragingly. "Do tell. But first let's decide on our order."

"That's easy," Nell said. "Oysters. And then maybe a crispy fish taco on the small plate."

"It's decided then," Robert said. "Please continue."

Nell began counting on her fingers.

"Well, there's document forgery. And literary forgery, which is really just a close cousin. Then there's currency forgery, but that's in a special category—that's called counterfeiting. Very technical and apparently Mr. Willoughby hasn't over-indulged in that."

She thought for a moment.

"But he has forged postage stamp cancellations. Cancellations increase the value of rare stamps," she explained in a kindly aside, in case Robert didn't know, "so that's sort of like counterfeiting."

Nell frowned and shook her head.

"It's all so confusing. Oh, and art forgeries; I forget about them and they are probably the most sophisticated and romantic kind of fraud, and those come in more varieties and flavors than I can name."

The waitress, wearing a gray tee shirt with the Brine logo, appeared with a smile, and Robert placed the order for oysters, adding in two glasses of a bright Willamette Valley Sauvignon Blanc to set them off.

"Then we'll follow with fish tacos," he instructed her.

Nell brightened.

"Oysters are brain food," she told Robert, "and I have to keep all this material straight. Okay, here's the definition of document forgery." She began reciting confidently. "It is the creation of a fake document or the alteration of a genuine one with the intent to defraud. That's the nut, Robert—intention. I guess it's okay to create or alter something as long as your intentions are honorable."

She caught Robert's smirk. He was having a good time at her expense, but Nell plunged ahead anyway.

"But how could your intentions be good," she asked, "if you were mucking about with a falsified document? Oh, well, never mind. If you fill in the blanks of a document that has a genuine signature, or if you materially alter or erase an existing document, that's forgery, as long as you were intending to defraud. Are you still with me, Robert?"

"Go on," he said. He had steepled this fingers and was tapping them against his chin in a characteristic Robert Hutchins gesture of thought and patience.

"The instruments of forgery," Nell instructed in lofty tones, "may include bills of exchange or bills of lading—I can never remember what bills of lading are. Forgery can apply to promissory notes, checks, bonds, receipts, orders for money or goods, mortgages or discharges of same, deeds, public records, accounts books, certain kinds of tickets or passes for transportation or events. *Whew!*"

She paused to draw a deep breath. But she wasn't through yet.

"Methods of forgery may include handwriting, printing, engraving or typing. But I gather it doesn't really become a crime until the forged document is offered as genuine."

Looking exhausted by recalling and reciting all this, Nell brushed back a strand of hair with the back of her hand and took a grateful sip of the wine that had suddenly materialized on the high table.

"Forgery is defined as a felony," she went on, "and it is usually considered as fraud, and punishment is generally a fine or imprisonment or both."

Nell took another deep breath.

"Now getting back to art forgery—that gets complicated. Works of art can be copied or replicated without any crime being charged. However, if someone attempts to sell the art or misrepresents it—claims it as original—then the copy becomes an illegal forgery. Also, and this is interesting—I learned this when I was researching a forger named Mark Landis—a *donated* work that is fake can't be prosecuted as forgery because money wasn't exchanged. This guy, Mark Landis, forged artwork from several centuries right up to the present, because he enjoyed playing philanthropist. He passed off his forgeries as the works of known artists and gifted them to museums all over the country. He duped dozens of curators and he never spent a day in prison."

"What kind of forgery does your Mr. Willoughby pursue?" Robert asked.

"I am just learning about that," Nell admitted humbly. "I know he first put his foot on the downward path of crime by forging identification that would allow young Harvard men to drink in public houses, but we have a long way to go before I know Mr. Willoughby's long history as a forger. Oh, here are the oysters. What a treat, Robert. Thank you for lunch and thank you listening."

CHAPTER 6

"Of course, technology has supplanted a lot of the work I used to do," H.H. Willoughby was saying. Nell was back in The Shop inside the old house in Newbury. She had made herself as comfortable as possible in the plush armchair Henry had provided, and the tiny red light showed the Sony was collecting information. Nell sat at attention.

"Stock certificates, for instance," Henry continued. "I used to do quite a brisk business altering stock certificates. Very lucrative. But," he mourned, "with the exception of some genteel ladies of my own vintage, very few people hold their own securities these days. Corporations have grabbed them up—'there, there, we'll just take care of that for you; you needn't bother.' And then the stockholders are only assured of their ownership if they get regular dividends or when the proxies come once a year begging for their votes."

Nell could sympathize.

"A shame, really," Henry continued. "Those certificates were beautiful things. Each a distinctive design. Each a work of art. You had one of those and you knew you really had something—something to touch. Something to hold onto."

Nell could see Henry's grief. But he continued.

"And diplomas. That's another thing that's gone. These days colleges and universities just whizz the forms through ink jet printers and spit out the graduates' names in Lucida Script or Edwardian. Where is the majesty in that, I ask you? Four years at university or years swotting away in medical school… thousands of dollars spent…and what do you get? A cheap piece of paper in a cheap frame to hang in your office."

Henry Willoughby was angry about this injustice, not to mention the crassness of technology's answer.

"A diploma,'" he instructed, "should be something holy. An individual's good name should be treated with the greatest respect. It should be rendered meticulously in best quality India ink that won't fade with time."

He turned brightly to Nell.

"I used to calligraph all the diplomas for Harvard Medical School, had you known that?"

Nell hadn't.

"Yes, they called on H.H. Willoughby when every June was about to roll around. Ah," he reminisced, "the paper stock in those days … a fine tooth to it. Harvard spared nothing in those days. Took the ink without spidering, the paper did. My pen used to veritably float. Even now, when I go into a doctor's office or a lawyer's office—although those attorney's diplomas aren't generally as nice—I look up at the wall and see my calligraphy. I've pointed out my work to several physicians and they've thanked me very kindly."

"You can recognize your work?" Nell asked naively.

The question scandalized the old gentleman.

"Of course! Each one is an offspring of my pen, of my heart. And the names—I remember each name too."

A thought struck him.

"Most of the diplomas I've done were legitimate, mind you, but not all were. Not always. Upon occasion, I received a request to create a diploma for... well...for an individual who had not graced the ivied halls of a particular institution. Or who had not acceptably completed the course work. Such was the case with Dr. Michael V. Karpinski.

"Young Karpinski was an aspiring gastroenterologist, but he kept failing his anatomy classes and thus missing various graduations. Finally, deciding enough was enough, he took matters into his own hands.

"He came to me and asked me to create his Harvard diploma. And I did it. Karpinski framed the confabulation and hung it in his office. I saw it when I was there."

"You went to his office?" Nell asked.

"Yes. I was experiencing considerable pain—colitis. I'd struggled with it for a long time but it just got worse and worse. I knew it was time to see a good gastroenterologist, so I..."

"You went to see Karpinski?" Nell was aghast. "*Doctor* Karpinski the charlatan? The man whose credentials you yourself forged? A man who wasn't a recognized, truly certified physician? You went for *treatment*?"

"Well, yes," said Henry mildly. "I knew him, you see."

Nell made a brushing motion in front of her face.

"Go on, go on—just tell me what happened."

"Well, Dr. Karpinski diagnosed a section of leaky bowel that had to come out or it would just continue to become inflamed and irritated, so I agreed to the surgery..."

But Nell, incredulous, interrupted again.

"You went under his *knife*? You put yourself through anesthesia and trusted this...this person who couldn't even pass college anatomy, to open you up and remove a section of colon?"

"Yes indeed, and the operation was successful too. And I'll tell you something else," he fixed Nell with an intent gaze. "I've never been troubled with colitis since. Michael V. Karpinski is a fine doctor and his diploma attests to it!"

CHAPTER 7

"Bunty, are you any good at math?"

Nell was leaning on the kitchen counter, and she had been leaning there for some time, pencil in hand, writing down sums and dividing and subtracting and starting over. She perceived Bunty Whitney as a potential savior when her neighbor came slamming through the back door.

"I used to be able to do long division," Nell continued querulously, "but the fourth grade was ages ago."

"They don't do long division any more," Bunty told her, shouldering Nell gently aside to look at the paper. "What are you trying to do anyway?"

"I'm trying to tame this recipe for corn chowder. The recipe makes vats of the stuff."

"Not a good sign." Bunty pronounced. "You're hiding aren't you. The forgery memoir isn't going well?"

"I am feeling a bit inundated with information," Nell admitted. "I'm doing a cram course on what forgery is and what it isn't, and I do need a break."

Bunty applied herself to the recipe problem.

"Twenty-two pounds of potatoes," she read aloud. She whistled. "Twelve cans of evaporated milk. Holy crow. Just use another recipe, why doncha?"

But no. This was Edna's Famous Friday Night Corn Chowder and Nell Bane wasn't about to substitute second rate.

"The sweet corn is just in," she told Bunty. "The farm stands all over Newbury and Newburyport are awash with it, and the new corn deserves Edna's recipe. I'm going to use fresh corn though, instead of the frozen niblets Edna had to use. There was nothing else she could do because she'd make it in December. It was the highlight of the church fair."

EDNA'S FRIDAY NIGHT CORN CHOWDER

22 pounds potatoes, cubed
5 pounds onions, diced
12 cans evaporated milk
12 cans cream-style corn
3 sticks butter
12 large bags frozen niblet corn
3 gallons whole milk
1 tsp sugar per pot
salt and pepper to taste.

On Thursday, divide the potatoes and onions as evenly as possible between three large pots which are the tops of double boilers. Thursday night, add enough water to each pot to just cover potatoes and onions. Boil until tender, watching to make sure nothing sticks to the bottom. Cool as much as possible before placing the refrigerator overnight.

On Friday noon, heat the potatoes and onions and add to each pot: 4 cans cream-style corn, 4 cans evaporated milk, 1 stick of butter, 1 gallon of milk, salt, pepper and sugar, and 4 large bags of frozen niblets corns defrosted. Heat over boiling water all afternoon, stirring frequently to keep from sticking.

Bunty took pity on Nell and took away her pencil.

"Here," she said, producing her cell phone and accessing the calculator. "Let's see if we can reduce these ingredients and still produce a passable chowder.

Nell's and Bunty's Version of Edna's Corn Chowder

3 large russet potatoes, diced
1 large yellow onion, chopped
2 12-oz. can evaporated milk
1 can cream-style canned corn
1/4 cup butter
4 cups whole milk
4 ears of butter-and-sugar corn, cut from the ears.

Combine onions and potatoes in a soup pot and add cold water just to cover. Bring to just to boiling, then simmer until potatoes are tender, stirring occasionally to prevent sticking. The following day, heat the potatoes and add cream-style corn, evaporated milk, butter and whole milk. Heat in double boiler for 2-3 hours.

Shortly before serving, melt 2T butter over medium-high heat in a non-stick skillet and toss in the kernels of sweet corn, stirring for no more than one minute. Scrape the kernels into the chowder and serve.

"Why not put the sweet corn in with the other stuff?" Bunty wanted to know.

But Nell was adamant. Sweet corn, she maintained, was fragile and susceptible to toughening.

"It would be better to use it absolutely raw than to overcook it," she claimed. "But it only should be cooked a tidge!"

"A tidge," Bunty repeated. "Got it."

CHAPTER 8

Ever since she'd blundered onto his name during her research, Nell had been intrigued by the forger Mark Landis. For Landis, the forged sketches and watercolors that he gifted to museums were simply means to his end, which was to pass himself off as a philanthropist. In that, Nell perceived, Landis's life was as phony as his art. But what had led Henry Willoughby into his own shady career? She decided to ask.

Henry chuckled when Nell wondered if he'd ever had aspirations similar to Landis's.

"Heavens no, my dear. Dear me, no. I simply liked to eat. Just a bowl of soup and a crust of bread and enough money in my checking account to pay the property taxes on the manse up in Newbury. I couldn't allow that to slip away on my watch. No."

Nell thought Henry seemed sad. She bit back the urge to comfort him though and waited in silence for him to enlarge on the subject of his dodgy career choice. Long experience as a ghostwriter had taught her the value of silence. "The first one to speak, loses" she often told herself. And now, her silence was rewarded.

"Back in Museum School days," Willoughby said, "I fancied myself as a painter of fine art, more in the realism school than in any of the contemporary movements like Cubism or Pointellism. And while I admit the contemporary scene was hot, still there was some market for my work, although not a large one, and often I did worry when the tax collector came calling. So when the opportunity to supplement my income appeared on my doorstep, I never slammed the door."

Henry Willoughby looked severely at Nell as if he were trying to make up his mind about something. Then, apparently, he decided to go ahead.

"There are many bad eggs in this world, my dear," he instructed. "You'd be surprised. As long as I kept my door open, a number of those eggs rolled in. There are people who want wills to be altered in order to cheat rightful heirs out of inheritances. There are criminals who wish documentation—passports and such—that will allow them to slip the nets of the law. I sometimes think that first false I.D. that I inked for Forsyth the Younger marked me—invested me with the scent of corruption. It was my fall from grace. My walking papers out of Eden. Potential customers knew I was imminently corruptible. After Forsyth the Younger, customers simply appeared. I never knew from whence they came and I never asked questions. And if they tried to offer too much explanation, I quickly shut them off. I didn't want to know. I used my pens to render their desires in whatever manner was necessary. Whatever was required—an antique document or letter or receipt of certification. I simply knew how to assemble the materials and apply my skill to make a forgery credible and a work of art. I produced altered wills and testaments, and

I will admit to taking pride in my product. It was work that very few could manage. I offered value. And I was paid for my daily bread and I was grateful too. Bread is bread."

A storyteller herself, Nell loved being told stories, and she settled back in Willoughby's itchy shop armchair, eager to hear more.

"Every career has a turning point though, doesn't it?" Willoughby continued, "and mine came when I walked into Pleisher Art Restoration on Newbury Street and was hired by old Milton Pleisher himself. Did you ever hear of Milton Pleisher?"

Nell shook her head.

"No. Well, I guess you wouldn't have. He's been dead these many years but Pleisher—Uncle Milty, the staff called him— was the genuine article. He'd learned the trade of art restoration back in Germany, and when the Nazis came calling, he escaped with nothing more than what was in his head. Oh, but what was in that head!"

Henry Willoughby, considering, shook his own head in amazement. "Milton Pleisher deserves an entire chapter in my memoir."

Nell was ready.

CHAPTER 9

"What sorts of art did you work on at Pleisher's?" Nell wanted to know.

She was back in The Shop, and glad to be, for outside—and throughout New England—a late summer nor'easter was on the rampage. She'd had quite a time driving down from Newburyport with roadside puddles swooshing up the sides of her car and occasionally taking control of the tires and sending Nell and the Saab aquaplaning. She was relieved to pull into Henry Willoughby's driveway and make a dash for the house.

The Shop was dimmer than usual though, thanks to the weather outside, and the elderly floor lamp was hard-pressed to shed illumination.

"It wasn't only art at Pleisher's," Henry told her. "We saw a lot of family documents. Baptismal certificates. Marriage licenses. Immigration papers. The interest in genealogy drove a lot of business Pleisher's way. People wanted to authenticate the history of their family's greatness. They wanted documentation. Military ephemera—enlistment papers, certificates of honor, honorable discharges. I never saw a dishonorable discharge though."

He permitted himself a quiet chuckle, then continued.

"Damaged photographs had to be repaired and restored. Cynthia Something was a whizz at that, but art restoration—that was Pleisher's forte. And since I was trained at the Museum School and had a modest representation with some works of my own hanging in a small gallery down at the less fashionable end of Newbury street, eventually Pleisher trusted me to work on the fine art that needed to be restored.

"He must have been in his eighties, Pleisher, when he hired me. And in my memory he is never standing upright. He was a heavy man—pear-shaped—and while his upper body seemed of normal size, from the sternum down, the rest of him bloomed out and descended into great slabs of flesh. His stomach rested on the lower parts and his great weight seemed to drag his shape downward so his hips overflowed the swivel chair on which he sat. It was a large chair, and fairly substantial—or would have been substantial had it not been so compromised by the burden it had been made to bear over the years. The chair creaked and protested and threatened to collapse. If it had—which it never did—it would have dumped its tenant onto the floor with a crash nothing short of seismic.

"Pleisher himself wasn't doing much of the art restoration by the time I came. Mostly he sat there at his table dribbling juices and dropping crumbs and directing his minions—and he could be quite dictatorial and often rude and crude. He sat there overseeing and overeating. He was a gourmand. Not a gourmet, you understand. No. He was a glutton. A *fresser*. In short, he was a pig. But he knew his stuff, mind you. In his own way, he was a genius, and people in Boston—and in New York too— knew he was the best, and they made their ways to

Newbury street."

Nell cleared her throat. "I'd like to know more about the practice of art restoration," she said. "I have only a hazy idea of what it's about and when and why it's done."

Henry Willoughby seemed gratified by her interest.

"Conservation is a better term," he told her, "restoration being only one branch of the art. Conservation involves the cleaning and stabilizing of art work which, if it is appropriately performed as preventive maintenance, then the intervention of restoration may not be necessary or at least not as extensive nor invasive."

He considered.

"There are those purists who'll argue that even cleaning should be avoided, for it may leave residue on the art that is inconsistent with the original media. I don't share that view however. Well, as a restorer, I wouldn't, would I?

"I view restoration as vital to the survival of classical artwork and if proper research is conducted, original colors and materials can be recognized and duplicated.

"To give the purists their due, however, early conservation and restoration methods scare the bejeesus out of modern day conservators. Old manuals advocate covering an entire painting in wood ash then wiping it off with water. This coated the painting in an extremely alkaline—and extremely harmful—substance. Shocking!

"No, modern approaches are much gentler. And here technology *is* a benefit. It is common practice now to use X-rays to see how the original was composed and the conservator gains understanding by analyzing the different absorption rates. And infrared imaging can show the original and can detect where paint is lost. And now there are fixed wavelength cameras that can pinpoint carbon-based drawings with distinctive wavelengths.

"Well, I could natter on and on about how conservancy and restoration has improved. Why, the subject of varnish alone could fill a textbook. But when I stumbled into Pleisher Art Restoration, it was still back in the Dark Ages of the art.

"Milton Pleisher, however, had some instinct—some usual gift—for analyzing a piece of art and for "seeing" its original form. His DNA seemed encoded with X-ray vision and he could apparently see with the vision of infrared imaging. He was a human spectrophotometer. He just knew. He diagnosed and prescribed and set us, his technicians, to work. Then, having finally finished breakfast and given his orders, he'd continue on to lunch.

"I was the third technician when I was hired. Low man on the totem pole. David Gomes was there before me. Terribly nervous man. Every time Uncle Milty barked an order, Gomes dropped whatever tool was in his hand. The racket made Uncle Milty madder and he'd yell all the louder. Gomes was with Pleisher for years until he resigned to commit suicide. Then there was Cynthia Something. Nice girl. As steady and unflappable as Gomes was nervous. She eventually quit to move to Framingham—*Framingham*—and have babies. That left only me, and I continued to toil on in Pleisher's employ and continued paying taxes to the town of Newbury in order to keep the fallow farm of long-dead Willoughbys off the town's delinquency rolls."

"What happened to Pleisher?" Nell wanted to know. "Did you ever resign? What did Uncle Milty say?"

"Milton Pleisher faded gradually," Henry Willoughby said. "He got older. The firm got crustier. Faded. Out-dated. And Pleisher himself got vaguer. Gomes was gone. Cynthia Something was gone, presumably populating the Framingham school system at warp speed. I was handling almost all of the firm's work then, but by that time, Stone was practically a fixture at Pleisher's. He was always hanging about, coming up with something for me to do, and I was working long hours and, I have to admit, building a tidy nest egg. I'd stopped worrying about those quarterly tax payments. Then one day Milton Pleisher fell over. By the time the EMTs arrived, he'd cashed in his chips. It was a swift end, and I believe a relatively painless one. The firm closed down. The inventory was auctioned off. I took a few things to which I felt somehow entitled, and I shifted back up to Newbury and set up The Shop. Full stop."

Henry Willoughby stopped talking and looked at Nell.

"Still awake?" he asked her. "I haven't bored you rigid yet, have I?"

"Not at all,"" Nell told him.

She sat up straighter in her chair though, and turned off the Sony. The tiny red light winked out.

"That's probably enough information for today though. You've given me a lot of material to absorb."

She stretched.

"Next time," Henry promised, "I'd like to return to the subject of the slippery slope. As we conclude this session, I will leave myself standing at the crossroads of a new career. And perhaps it is time to introduce you to Woodford Stone."

Henry flashed his elfin grin. Was it her imagination, or had Nell seen him actually wiggle his ears?

CHAPTER 10

Nell was auditioning titles for Henry Willoughby's memoir. She had offered him several options but at each suggestion, he shook his head. Nothing seemed to suit, and Nell feared her creative juices were drying up. Then inspiration flashed.

"Henry," she said, "what do you think of this? *My Place in the Gallery of Rogues: A Forger's Memoir.*"

Henry Willoughby cocked his head to one side, considering. He looked to Nell like a bright-eyed little bird—a chickadee. Henry tried it out. Then he tried it out again.

"Yes!" he cried. "I think that could work. Could work very well. I'm seeing framed portraits as if hanging in a museum. All the greats are there: Wolfgang Beltracchi, Han van Meegeren. Guy Ribes, and hanging right there with them, none other than Henry Herbert Willoughby! A fine company of thieves."

He laughed with delight.

"Brilliant. You are a wonder my dear."

Nell tried to look modest, but in fact she was relieved. Now, with the title accepted, she could begin to unwind Henry's story.

My Place in the Gallery of Rogues:
A Forger's Memoir
H.H. Willoughby

I never intended to wander down the path of deceit and deception by following the career of a forger. No, it wasn't intentional. For a long while, I didn't even consider myself a forger. I was simply pursuing the career I'd trained for—a career in fine art—and I'd hoped and expected my chosen path would supply me with a living wage. But as each stroke of pen or brush carried me further along, the path began to diverge, like Robert Frost's road in the yellow wood, and I—well, I chose the path less traveled by—and the one more treacherous.

Each forger has unique reasons for pursuing his career, and fortune, believe it or not, is not always the most compelling one.

Psychologists who study these things claim that most forgers are motivated at first by failure. Having entered the art world, bright with anticipation, they didn't encounter the success they'd expected and felt they deserved. So, surprised and very often angry, they turned their not inconsiderable talents in other directions. And I must admit that in some measure, this description applies to me.

Sometimes there is a passive-aggressive motive of revenge against the art community that judged them not "good enough." There's an I'll-get-even attitude that accuses the art experts, curators and even collectors of conspiring to negate an artist's talent. And this drives some forgers to seek revenge by passing off their own original work as the work of recognized artists or by duplicating the work of highly successful ones.

They seek retribution by embarrassing or unmasking the experts in the art community, and they derive great satisfaction when a forgery is revealed and the experts appear to come up short or are even recognized as charlatans themselves. There's also the satisfaction of demonstrating that they are good artists after all—good enough to pass for the best. And even if the deceit is never recognized—well, the smug secret is safe and the forger can paint another day. And of course, there's also the consolation prize of the cash.

Some us in in the brotherhood are thrill seekers addicted to flirting with danger and to dancing on the razor's edge of discovery—the moment when the deception is revealed. Or we crave the adrenaline rush when the fraud isn't detected and we've slipped the noose of detection one more time.

Then there are others who don't crave that particular thrill and who actually want to be caught. Or so say some psychologists, and surely they should know. Some forgers only gain the fame they crave after they have endured the trial by fire of prison or public scorn. Ken Perenyi was largely unknown until, in retirement, he published his memoir *Caveat Emptor* and *The New York Times* brought him fame in a profile, calling him America's greatest forger.

A few of us tease. Until a forger's provenance comes to light, the works stand as authentic but the teaser enhances the game of detection by dropping hints into the work—clues that the art is forged. "Time bombs" is the term forger Tom Keating invented, and he deliberately used titanium white pigment in his paintings—a medium that hadn't been invented when many of the originals were painted. Catch me if you can. And if you can't, shame on you.

Some forgers live to put one over on the art experts, the certifiers of authenticity, and the art collectors who so willingly pay thousands for a "name" to hang on their walls. Each sale is a triumph—a silent cry of "Ha! Not as smart as you think!" Each is proof that the forger's talent is the equal of the original artist's hand.

Well, all those reasons, and probably more, have led competent artists and otherwise decent people, to put a foot on the road less taken. And...as they say...the money ain't so bad either.

And so I, Henry Herbert Willoughby, retired now, and modestly successful, hang my shingle in the Rogues' Gallery of Forgers—a good old fashioned league in the medieval artisan's tradition. And reverently—nodding respectfully as I go—I tiptoe down the hall of this fine company of thieves.

"How do you do Mr. Beltracchi? You certainly enjoyed embarrassing art evaluators and sophisticated art collectors. And you didn't do so badly for yourself either—apart from that unfortunate stint in the slammer, of course. And those stories of unloading the collections of wealthy grandparents— well, that completely duped those greedy curators and collectors who were looking to make a killing on masterpieces. Nice work, Wolfgang."

"Ah, John Myatt, I think I've walked your path. There you were, toiling in your studio, trying to support your family with your paintings and taking on students for what little they could pay. Maybe you were born in the wrong era, John, for your pastoral style, though charming, just wasn't in step with the raw contemporary paintings that collectors were clamoring for. Still, there were those children to feed, and there was nothing illegal in your scheme to sell "genuine fakes." You were quite up front about it. Nothing duplicitous in that. But you have to hold your friends close, John, and your enemies closer—as I found out myself—and we were both drawn across the line of legality."

"Good day, Mr. Landis. And who are you today? A Jesuit

priest, perhaps? Or just an average run-of-the-mill philanthropist taking pleasure from conning curators and caging a free meal in exchange for the gift of a swiftly, although skillfully, rendered sketch or watercolor?"

"And Herr van Meergeren. I bow to you, sir. Like so many of us, an insulted ego propelled you into greatness. You got even by forging paintings from the Dutch Golden Age, and so successfully too, that after the war—and after your trial, of course (where you defended yourself brilliantly, by the way)—you became a national hero when it was revealed that your forged Vermeer had duped none other than Hermann Goring."

So here I stand at the far end of the gallery. My forger's career is behind me and the pleasure of writing my memoir is just ahead. Yes, I chose the road less traveled by, and as the poet noted, that has made all the difference.

Henry Herbert Willoughby

CHAPTER 11

"What does his artwork look like?" Bunty Whitney wanted to know. "His own artwork, I mean. Does he do landscapes? Portraits? Wild Jackson Pollock-looking stuff? What?"

"Gosh, Bunty," Nell was shocked. "You know, I've never directly asked him. There's stuff all over The Shop but I've never looked at it that closely. Never asked if it was original and what was part of the forgery oeuvre."

Full of determination to correct this oversight, Nell marched into The Shop exactly on time for their next memoir session. There was someone in The Shop, however, and Nell took a step back in surprise.

The man sitting in the itchy armchair—her chair—turned his face slowly to her, but Henry immediately slid off his stool. He small feet hit the floor with a double bump.

"Nell!"

He seemed surprised to see her, but they'd made this date. Surely she was expected?

"Come in, come in, my dear. There is someone you should

meet."

His eyes returned to his guest. The man, Nell thought, had been watching Henry the way a cat watches a bird at a feeder. She felt a shiver prickle at the back of her neck. Now the man rotated his gaze toward her and slowly—very slowly—uncrossed his long legs and languidly, as if it were an exhausting effort, pulled himself to his feet, gradually straightening his spine into his considerable height.

"Mrs. Bane—Nell—this is Woodford Stone, my associate." Henry said. He coughed.

"Nell, please," she said, stepping close enough to Stone to present her outstretched his hand. She had the impression that he was considering whether or not to accept it.

"How do you do?" he finally asked.

Woodford Stone was impressively tall and casually but expensively dressed. His eyes were dark—like anthracite—and if they had any depth, Nell couldn't detect it. They were like the lenses of sunglasses, those eyes, reflecting back the viewer's face and revealing nothing of the mind working behind the eyes. Nell didn't believe in auras and energies—or so she usually claimed—but if she were a believer, she'd say this man had a black aura. A negative aura that repelled. Slightly offended, she stepped away from him, anxious to put space between herself and Woodford Stone's polarizing energy field.

"So you work with Henry?" she asked politely.

"On occasion," Stone replied languidly. He looked pointedly at Willoughby, sarcastically adding, "When he *deigns* to work, that is."

"I've retired, Woodford," Henry said defensively. "I've told you that. I explained that."

"Unacceptable answer, Willoughby. You can't—you can never— just walk away from this."

Nell wondered what it was that Henry wasn't supposed to

walk away from, and she looked to her friend for some explanation. But Henry was firmly shaking his head.

"No, Woodford. I've told you no and I mean it. This time I mean it."

"An opportunity like this one may never come up again," Stone said. "Well, I'll leave you to mull it over and perhaps come to your senses, which you will certainly do when you've seen the value in it."

He passed the radar dish of his dark gaze across Nell, as if trying to decide whether to be civil to her or not. In the end, he gave her a curt nod, raised a hand in a limpid salute to Henry and stepped through the door.

Woodford Stone's exit seemed to take with it all the oxygen in the room. Henry Willoughby and Nell stood facing each other, each trying to regulate their breathing, each grasping for some emotional railing to support normalcy.

Nell recovered first.

"Well. Before we begin, Henry, I really want to see some your paintings. Real H.H. Willoughby art."

Henry was pleased.

"I've nothing in The Shop," he told her, "but out in the manse I have several small oils that I'm told are rather good."

Nell followed him, treading along so carefully on the narrow burlap trails in the ancient rugs, that she nearly trod on Henry's heels when he stopped abruptly in front of portrait of a sweet child who looked to be about twelve. Expecting landscapes—bucolic scenes of local salt marshes and orchards where a few cows grazed—she was surprised.

"I never knew you did portrait," she cried. "How marvelous. I'm impressed."

Henry was modest.

"Not just anyone can do figure," Nell insisted. "I have a dear friend up in Newburyport—Ann Fitzmaurice—who paints portraits so I know something of the challenge portrait presents."

"I know of Mrs. Fitzmaurice, but only by reputation. We've never met. Although," Henry added shyly. "I'd like to meet her."

"This is the study for a portrait of Julia Smithfield," he told Nell. "At her mother's request, I painted it in the style of John Singer Sargent. The final work hangs in her parents' home in Gloucester."

Nell was struck.

"It has real energy," she said. "I feel like this child has just run in from playing on the beach—all windblown and rosy with sunburn. She looks like a perfectly delightful child on a perfect summer day."

Henry Willoughby rocked from toe to heel and back again. His hands in his trouser pockets clinked bits of metal—coins and perhaps a tiny pocket knife or pillbox. Nell's delight seemed to please him. And Nell, for her part, looked at her client with new appreciation and respect.

"We've got work to do," she told him energetically. "We have to get your story told. We've got to take that memoir to market!"

CHAPTER 12

"Just who is Woodford Stone?" Nell asked, when they were back in The Shop with a pot of tea and two bone china cups on a tray. "You said he is your associate?"

"*Was* my associate," Willoughby replied. "Since my retirement, I think the association should be spoken of in the past tense."

Nell was silent for a moment.

"He didn't seem to accept your claim of retirement," she finally observed.

"Nor will he, as long as there is an opportunity to promote another forgery. And to profit from it."

Nell thought she heard a note of bitterness in Henry's statement. Once again she played the ghostwriter's trump card of silence and waited.

"A forger almost always needs an accomplice, my dear," he told her, "although Woodford, like most, would bridle at the label."

He sighed, as if agreeing to a confession.

"The accomplice is most often a certifier—an expert, although often a self-styled one and sometimes one whose veracity is as questionable as the artwork the experts will eventually try to unmask. But there has to be someone who can present the forgery and attest to its authenticity. Someone who vouches for its provenance. The certifier meets with the prospective buyers—that is with the museum curator or the gallery owner or even with the collector who is keen to make an impressive purchase. He brokers the deal. He's the salesman. He's the hands-on guy so the artist can stay safely in hiding."

Nell was silent, considering this.

Henry Willoughby helped her out.

"Not all forgery is fraud," he told her. "I might produce a painting in the style of a well known artist—Edward Hopper, let's say, or Andrew Wyeth perhaps. It's a matter of researching the artist's media and technique, but it requires something more. It requires the painter to know the artist's hands. There has to be a real instinct for how that individual paints, and in that, I've always believed, resides the true genius of the forger.

"Now here's where it gets gray. Instead of forging Hopper's name or Wyeth's, Stone would present the painting simply as "in the style of Hopper". The buyer would go ahead with the purchase, hoping that his guests, recognizing the original artist's 'hand' would infer its pedigree. As long as no one claimed the piece was the work of another, there is no implication of fraud."

Nell frowned and shook her head.

"This is all so complicated," she complained.

Henry Willoughby sighed.

"Well, let's go back to the beginning—to the ancient history Woodford Stone and I share—and we'll see if we can clear the mud from this puddle."

Once again Nell watched Willoughby reel back his mind through time. He'd apparently picked a date.

"I had been with Pleisher for some years when I met Stone. I was restoring documents for the most part—and I must say I took considerable pleasure in cleaning up and brightening the awards and family papers of Pleisher's customers and clients. They were always so grateful. So thrilled with the result. That is very rewarding in and of itself, my dear—the approbation of clients. It's like applause to an actor on opening night. The remuneration is just the cherry on the whipped cream.

"So I enjoyed what I was doing for the most part, and the hours at Pleisher's left a little time in the evenings for my own paintings. You might say I was even prolific, in a modest way. There was a little gallery at the far west end of Newbury street— long gone now and its name is swallowed in time—but the proprietor liked my style and allowed me to hang in the shop. And from time to time, some paintings sold, then he and I would split the take."

Henry smiled reminiscently.

"Then I'd split my half between the accrual account on the property taxes and a dinner at the Parker House.

"Well, Pleisher was always very careful about who he allowed to work on his art restorations. Very discriminating. But eventually he granted me permission to clean some paintings, then gradually he promoted me to doing touch-ups—actual bits of restoration. By the time Gomes exited the shop—and the earth, for that matter—I had become Uncle Milty's go-to boy."

As Nell watched, Henry turned his gaze ceiling-ward once more. She was recognizing this as his trick for recalling dates.

"Ah! Yes."

He had it.

"Years ago. Twenty, probably, maybe thirty, I'd say. Yes. That's when Woodford Stone started coming into Pleisher's. He seemed to know Milton from some earlier time, but I didn't pay much attention. And he certainly didn't pay any attention to *me*. Among his other faults and attributes, Woodford is something of a snob.

"Well after some time, and after he'd become a familiar figure, I learned that Stone was considered an expert in establishing provenance. His name was well known and he was respected.

"Let me explain why this is important, my dear. Just as it is important for breeders of fine race horses to intimately know their thoroughbreds' pedigrees, so is it essential to everyone in the art community—everyone who buys, sells or collects— to establish the provenance of every treasure they contemplate purchasing. Or in some cases, to winnow out the fakes before they buy. Provenance includes establishing legal title. It's much like the Registry of Motor Vehicles, Nell. A legal title is essential to keep you within the law as well as for protection. Simply put, provenance must be established for three reasons: for authenticity, for valuation, for ownership.

"I think, in the beginning, Woodford Stone was an upright, legitimate certifier of artwork. I'd like to believe he subscribed to the guidelines of the International Foundation for Art Research. He was knowledgeable in his subject and honest in his dealings. Well...that's what I'd like to believe.

"But like Lucifer, Woodford Stone fell from Grace and fell from Heaven. He started crossing the line of legitimacy.

"At first Stone paid me no mind. I'd nod to him courteously, then put my head down over my work, but slowly, gradually at first, Stone would stroll by my work table and glance over my shoulder at the document I was restoring. I'd hear him grunt from time to time, but I never did hear him

54

snort."

Henry grinned.

"A grunt, for your information Nell, is an approbation. A snort expresses derision."

Nell smiled. "Please continue," she said.

"I gather Stone started to talking to Pleisher about me, and I guess Milton wasn't completely dismissive. And Stone must have squirreled away in his head the information that I was a a credible document guy and maybe more. And while I didn't know it at the time, he was planning to use me to forge certain documents of certification. Documents that would supply provenance to works that...well...weren't deserving."

Henry's face clouded as he moved aside the curtains of the past.

"I'm not proud of this next thing," he said.

Suddenly he looked directly at Nell.

"But if this memoir is going to be genuine—authentic—then I must tell it."

Nell smiled empathetically

"If it is to have *provenance*," she supplied.

Henry Willoughby beamed.

"Exactly. Therefore I shall confess. Well, it happened at a dismal moment in my financial picture. Through a perfect storm of household events, I was required to fund a new roof on the manse and a new oil burner in its cellar."

Henry's blue eyes grew wide, incredulous even at the memory.

"There was nothing to do but write the checks for the work even though my account was all but depleted, and I was uncertain whether those checks would clear. Then the quarterly real estate tax bill landed on my desk. At that moment, my savior arrived in the unlikely form of Woodford Stone.

"He was near to closing a deal with a museum director

who was hot to get some painting or other into a collection, and all Woodford needed was some paperwork documenting the legitimacy of the painting."

Henry looked pained.

"It was phony, of course. And Stone knew it. But all it would take was a signature. A forged signature on a line at the bottom of the paper, and Stone was dangling enough money to satisfy the tax collector down at Newbury Town Hall. And I did it. I picked up the pen and I took the money. And from that time forward, I was something—someone—I hadn't been before. I had crossed a line."

CHAPTER 13

"Now where were we? Henry asked.

"You had forged a signature," Nell prompted, "and you said you'd crossed a line."

"Yes. Yes, indeed. Well, the die was cast, as Caesar said. *Alea iecta est.* Woodford Stone knew he had me."

He looked brightly at Nell.

"Do you remember that story '*The Devil and Daniel Webster*'?"

"Stephen Vincent Benet, wasn't it? Yes."

"Well then, you'll remember how the main character in that story struggled with his fields and his family and had a troubling mortgage to pay. Nothing was going well for the poor fella and one day he looked around and said: 'I vow it's enough to make a man want to sell his soul to the devil! And I would, too, for two cents.'"

Nell was smiling.

"And the very next day," she supplied, "who should come calling but Old Scratch."

Now Henry Willoughby was nodding.

"Exactly so. In my modest little life, the devil didn't wear black boots and carry a collecting box—at least not one I could see—but he came for me alright. Came in smooth city clothes. Came in polished upper class tones. And for a few dollars, to pay that mortgage bill, I sold him my soul."

"Now Henry," Nell counseled. "Surely it wasn't that dramatic."

And Henry Willoughby laughed.

"You caught me! And you're right. I have free will. Strapped as I was, I could have said no. And I have to say the ride has been grand. I've enjoyed most of it, and I've escaped to retire comfortably and so far my soul hasn't been put in the devil's collection box. Although..."

And here Henry twinkled.

"...although I sometimes wonder about Mr. Woodford Stone's soul. But to get back to my story.

"Quite by happenstance, Stone stopped into that little gallery that carried a few of my paintings. Well, maybe it wasn't happenstance. It was his business to get around and sniff out artwork of all kinds. Not much escaped that nose either. And Woodford picked up on the familiar signature that is mine, and he had a few words with the gallery owner, and then he paid a call on me, much the way the devil paid a call on that hapless New Hampshire farmer."

Henry smiled, remembering, but this time the smile was rueful.

"It was a different fella who came calling into Pleisher's. All smiles he was. 'How are you, Henry?' 'Pleasant day isn't it?' 'Are you planning a vacation this year, Henry? Any trips upcoming?'

"Well, right away I knew something was up. Stone invited me out to dinner, and like a fool, I accepted. We went to the Parker House. Nothing was too good for Henry Willoughby that night, and Stone ordered a bottle of wine. Good wine. Good enough for the sommelier to bring it and pour it out for Stone to taste. Stone sampled it and pronounced it good enough for his good friend Willoughby. And I? I sat there gullible as a bumpkin from Newbury, letting myself be conned.

"We talked a lot about my style. To whom did I compare my painting? Mark Rothko? Well, no, of course not. Klee? No, nothing modern. I could do it, of course, but it didn't interest me. Well then, the old boys; Renoir, Matisse, the Dutch masters? Uh...maybe. Yes. Sure.

"Let's see—let's see you back up that claim. That's what Stone said. He challenged me. And so we started. He directed me just as if he were an art director in a Newbury street agency. Gave me assignments, and he paid me for them too.

"Well, that was a pretty good deal I thought. Anytime I wasn't working at Pleisher's I was painting away in my studio using every trick in my kit to reproduce works by other artists, both major and minor. Stone would chuckle and pay me and carry most of the paintings away and I'd never see them again. Sometimes I felt like a new mother who puts a baby up for adoption and never even gets to hold it.

"For a while I never asked Stone what he did with the paintings. Then I got curious one day and I did ask.

"He was vague. Told me not to worry, that I hadn't signed the paintings and there was nothing to implicate me. That tinkled a little bell of alarm. Up to then, I hadn't been worried.

"So I poked around a little myself and discovered Stone was selling the paintings, and leveraging his reputation as a *bona fide* art certifier to do it. He had a little black book full of curators and museum directors and gallery owners, and he had personal acquaintanceships with some serious and influential collectors as well. Woodford Stone was doing very well for himself.

"For the glutton, however, nothing is ever enough. He started hatching a heist scheme. Do you know what that is, Nell?"

Thinking of the great Gardner Museum heist of 1990, Nell attempted a hesitant definition.

"It's where thieves try to swap a piece of recognized and valuable art for a forged copy, and with luck the fake won't be recognized. Is that about right?"

"It is, but if you're remembering the Gardner case, the scoundrels didn't even bother to substitute, they just snatched. Cut those valuable masterpieces out of their frames, and to this day, the frames hang empty in the Gardner's galleries.

"No. Stone wasn't planning anything as ambitious as the Gardner heist, not did he have his eye on anything as famous and valuable as the Vermeer that was taken or Rembrandt's *The Storm At Sea*. But there was a gallery in Boston that had a valuable Murdoch—just a small oil, mind you. Easy enough to swap and spirit out if the timing were just right. I was familiar with the painting and with Murdoch's technique. Andrew Murdoch wasn't all that great shakes as a painter anyway, if you want my opinion, so I thought what the hell. I threw caution to the winds one night, and using the photo from the gallery's catalog, I phonied up the painting and forged the squib that was Murdoch's signature. I let the thing dry and Stone carried it away. That was that. The very week after the swap out, a client walked into the gallery and paid a packet for the painting. Of course the gallery and Murdoch got the money. Neither Stone nor I got a thing. I didn't anyway, but here's what Stone got—he got the information that I could handle a forgery as delicate and dicey as that was. He learned we could dupe the experts. And he'd learned he had the stuff—the brazen guts— that could carry off a heist."

Forgery's Partner
Excerpt from My Place in the Gallery of Rogues
from H.H. Willoughby's Memoir

Most forgers don't operate alone. We may work in a studio or at a desk but either way, we almost always depend on someone on the outside—a partner in crime. We need a front man to handle our work, to broker it and to make the sales. This person needs credentials, of course, and some of these credentials— probably most—are real. Or they were real once upon a time until they were compromised by avarice. In my case, the accomplice was Woodford Stone.

Stone was a brilliant man, I always thought. Keen of mind, quick of wit. He could, if he chose, be amusing, but he rarely chose. The same could be said of his charm. Stone had the benefit of a fine education. Yale School of Art, I think, and he had studied abroad at the Tate Gallery. He had traveled in august art circles, meeting people and hob-knobbing and collecting names to later drop. His polished manners and handsome face made him memorable and his education and his membership in IFAR made him credible.

I don't know what corrupted Woodford Stone, but I suspect greed was most of it. The money was just too good, but I also think he had a gambler's love of the game. If there was a game to be had, a chance to outwit someone or put something over on someone else, Stone wanted to be in on it.

In the beginning, Woodford Stone was my mentor. He became my nemesis.

CHAPTER 14

Newburyport's popular 12 Center, after an unfortunate stint as a restaurant of a different name, had fortunately reopened as Brick & Ash, and the city's citizens had hurried back in. Nell was relieved to see the white brick walls had been sandblasted and returned to the original mottled red. The restaurant was billing itself as a casual spot to dig in and hang out, serving up comfort food and smoky barbeque, and Nell was planning to hang out with Bunty Whitney and Ann Fitzmaurice. They intended to combine a light supper with a sort of business meeting, for they were trying to establish a craft guild in Newburyport. Having arrived first, Nell chose a high table that overlooked Center Street on one side and the charming barroom on the other.

"Nell's new memoir client is in your line of work," Bunty told Ann when the women had squirmed onto chairs at the high table across from Nell.

Ann's attention swung toward Nell.

"Really? Tell me."

And so Nell did. When she got to the part about forgery though, Ann looked shocked, and Bunty, having achieved the effect she'd hoped for, smirked in satisfaction. But at that moment the waiter, who introduced himself as Jonathan, appeared and asked for their drink orders.

Ann and Nell each ordered a glass of white wine but Bunty requested a recitation of available beers. This required Jonathan to draw a deep breath and begin a long recitation.

"On tap, let's see—Poperings Hommel Belgian ale, Riverwalk IPA, Guinness stout (of course), Rising Tide Daymark Pale Ale, Jack's Abby Rotating Tap, Notch Brewing Rotating Tap…"

Bunty's satisfaction deepened as she considered all the choices that were possible before deciding on Riverwalk IPA.

As Jonathan departed, Ann instantly homed in again on the forger. As a portraitist of some standing on the North Shore, Ann was fascinated, and no, she had not heard of H.H. Willoughby although Nell assured her that Henry was a more than credible fine artist—in addition to being successful forger, of course.

"I thought we were getting together to talk about the Guild." Bunty crisply brought the conversation around to the reason the women had agreed to meet.

Ann and Nell rapidly shifted gears to address the challenge.

The Backstreet Guild was a loose affiliation of artists and artisans, professionals as well as talented amateurs, who were trying to establish a shop in Newburyport to sell their goods. Ann Fitzmaurice, known for her portraits, was a leading force in recruiting painters, and Bunty Whitney, with an established reputation and a flourishing list of customers, was heading up the pottery segment. For her part, Nell was supplying encouragement and, when specifically asked for it, advice.

"We need someone to head fiber arts," Ann said decisively.

They subsided into mutual thought.

"How about Moira Lester?"

"Macramé?" Bunty was incredulous. "That went out with love beads and *Laugh In*."

"Then what about Elsie Osborne?" Nell suggested. "Her quilts are amazing."

"She should certainly be invited," Ann said, "but I'd like to see someone who weaves. On looms, you know."

They considered further. This required a generous sampling of drinks.

"Joan Colcheccio? She weaves, doesn't she?"

Nell was making a list. As each of them thought of a local talent, Nell jotted down the name. Then she had a brilliant thought.

"Henry Willoughby! I'll bet he'd contribute a painting or two."

Her suggestion was greeted with a staggered silence.

"What?" she asked innocently.

"A forger?" Ann asked faintly. "Is that...I mean, is that ethical?"

Nell bristled.

"He's good, Ann. Very good. And he wouldn't submit a forgery. We'd ask for a genuine, signed Henry Herbert Willoughby painting."

"Go for it," Bunty was decisive. "We won't advertise him as a forger. He'll just be a guy from Newbury whose art will hang on the shop's walls. Now listen. I want the Smokehouse brisket. Are you two ready to order?"

CHAPTER 15

"Henry, now we need to roll back time even further. Time to tell me something of your childhood."

Henry Willoughby pawed his bald head for several moments. Then he yanked on the sprouts of white hair north of his ears.

"Not much to tell," he said finally. "Not much of interest anyway. But let's see... well, the Willoughby family manse was rather isolated. Especially then. It had been farmed for years but I guess in my grandfather wasn't much of a farmer, and he let the pasturage go to burdock and mugwort. Pa—that's what we called him—sold off quite a few acres; then my father sold off some more. All those tract houses you see attest to that. But there's still a lot of acreage attached to the manse, and of course with the sea so near, the old place is worth something. Hence the steep tax assessment."

Nell waited.

"As I say, it was isolated, so growing up, it was just me and Muriel."

"Who is Muriel?" Nell wanted to know.

"My younger sister, Muriel Willoughby. Muriel Willoughby Boudreau now. She lives in France, if you will. *Ohh-la-la!* Married a French fella—a wealthy one—and she lives in semi-luxury in the south of France."

Henry laughed.

"Old Muriel in France. That's a good one. I always think of her with a dirty face and torn stockings. As soon as Mother got her cleaned up, out she'd go again to climb a tree or jump in the hayloft or start picking blackberries, and she'd come in all scratched and stained, her pinafore torn to ribbons."

Henry smiled reminiscently.

"Old Muriel. Haven't seen her for years. I'd like to though."

"Why don't you go to France and see her?" Nell suggested. "You're retired now, you can do it."

"Naw. No, I guess not," Willoughby said slowly. "I guess it's too late."

Nell was slightly puzzled by this statement, still she let it pass. She waited for Henry to elaborate.

"At some point—but I mustn't have been very old—my Aunt Helen or someone gave me a watercolor set and a block of paper, and from that day forward the only thing I wanted to do was paint and draw. I'd go out into the fields and salt marshes and paint—I didn't know it was called *plein air*. I didn't care if I was chewed to bits by greenheads or if my feet were soaked at the end of the day as long as I had a few paintings that seemed to me worthwhile."

Henry was silent for a while, and Nell allowed him the space to think.

"From those days in the salt marshes, my path was clear," Henry continued. "I set my sights on the Museum School at the MFA and built my portfolio toward that goal and in the end, I was juried in. My, that was a grand day—the day I got my acceptance letter. I knew on that day, that I was going to be a great artist."

CHAPTER 16

For the ninth time Nell peeked in the Aga and checked the turkey. Simmering a stockpot of soup on the Aga's top side was one thing, but trusting to its guts an eighteen-pound bird, not to mention inviting six people over to dine on the result, was considerably more daring and stress-making. Nell was now asking herself the question that generations of hostesses have asked: "What in the world ever possessed me to invite these people over for dinner?" For in exactly forty-five minutes, they were all due to descend. Robert Hutchins, and Jerry Gasso of course, were even now driving up Route 95 from Beacon Hill with bottles of the new Beaujolais and Jerry's bourbon cranberry sauce—powerful and impossible to resist. Bunty was coming, naturally, and bringing pumpkin pie. Nell wondered if Bunty would remember the whipped cream. Ann and Franklin Fitzmaurice had been invited, and Ann had volunteered her famous buttery dinner rolls. And in a moment of inspiration, Nell had asked Henry Willoughby.

Henry was surprised, and apparently touched, by Nell's

invitation to Thanksgiving dinner.

"I don't receive many invitations, my dear," he had said, after running several passes over his bald head with both hands and tugging on the side tufts. "Dear me, I can't even remember the last time I was asked out. I shall hardly know how to behave."

"Not to worry," Nell told him stoutly, "I'll seat you beside me and murmur to you which fork to use."

The turkey wasn't turning the heavenly golden brown that it had in Nell's imagination, but it smelled delicious anyway. The whole house was redolent of it, thanks to the giblets simmering on the Aga's reliable surface. So Nell murmured a small but heartfelt prayer as she basted the turkey, and she closed the oven door.

They all arrived at once, and the decibel level in the little house was instantly impressive.

"Where's this Mr. Willoughby?" Jerry Gasso demanded. "You promised I would meet him, Nell, and I've begun to think you've reneged on the deal."

Jerry was looking all around as though Nell had hidden Willoughby and the fellow was going to pop out of a teapot at any moment like a genie.

"Yes." Bunty joined Jerry. "Are you sure he's coming? Did you confirm?"

Nell calmed their fears. "He'll be here in a few minutes, I'm sure. He just has to come from Newbury."

And Henry Willoughby, fortunately, put truth to Nell's promise. He arrived on the doorstep, wearing an astonishing bowtie and looking as elfin as he had when Nell first opened the door to him. Henry was holding a bunch of flowers—Stargazer lilies, unaccountably.

Nell was touched, although she did think her friend might have confused the seasons somewhat and that mums might have been more appropriate for Thanksgiving rather than Easter flowers.

"Oh, they smell heavenly," she exclaimed, burying her nose in the bouquet.

"Well, I had some difficulty scouting them up," Henry admitted, "but I knew what I wanted and I was very insistent. They kept trying to sell me *mums*," he added peevishly.

As Nell drew Henry Willoughby into the house, she was startled to find her other guests standing in a perfect semicircle, alert and eager to meet the honest-to-goodness forger. She recovered quickly and made the introductions.

As she presented Ann Fitzmaurice, Henry kissed Ann's hand.

"I admire your work very much indeed, Mrs. Fitzmaurice. I saw your painting *Summer Kissed* at the North Shore gallery. Congratulations. It richly deserved its prize."

Ann was shy but she was also gracious.

"And I, Mr. Willoughby, am extremely eager to learn about your work."

The two artists beamed at one another and settled in shortly to a discussion of squirrel mops and Winsor Newton oils with Jerry and Bunty eavesdropping avidly.

The turkey, in the end, did not disappoint. It transformed itself into a golden-brown holiday bird worthy of a food stylists dream, and Robert Hutchins carved it with surgical finesse. Franklin Fitzmaurice moved about the dining room table pouring the wine and filling the water goblets, while Jerry put the finishing touches on the cranberry sauce which involved pouring a scandalous amount of Kentucky bourbon over the hot and popping berries. As the scent of bourbon and fruit filled the air, Jerry cackled like a mad wizard over a cauldron.

Nell directed her guests to their seats and offered a heartfelt grace of thanks for each of them. At her request, Robert read

John Berryman's *Minnesota Thanksgiving—for that free Grace bringing us past great risks & thro' great griefs surviving to this feast...*

Conversation was lively and happy as dishes of vegetables went 'round and Ann's rolls were praised. Nell, checking frequently on her little guest from Newbury, saw happily that Henry Willoughby was an animated part of all conversation.

Nell finished her slice of pumpkin pie, and contently sipping her coffee, reflected that the meal and Berryman's poem had both ended the same: *Yippee!*

And Bunty remembered the whipped cream.

CHAPTER 17

Bunty Whitney, coming to collect her pie plates, found Nell unwrapping the turkey carcass that she and Ann had bundled into cling film the day before.

"Ah ha! That's why you invited all of us for Thanksgiving," Bunty accused. "So you could have the carcass to make soup."

Nell refused to rise to the bait.

"It's a bonus," she agreed, beginning to crack the bones and jam them into the stockpot. "How'd you think yesterday went? Did you like Henry Willoughby?"

Bunty took one of her own pottery mugs from a shelf and helped herself to coffee. These were the sorts of questions she could settle into the way another woman might squirm into a mink coat.

"Actually, I did. He was darling, and at first I just wanted to pinch his rosy little cheeks. But then, when he started talking, here comes this erudite, well-informed, perfectly delightful conversationalist. I was charmed. Completely won over."

Nell was gratified. Bunty Whitney rarely gave a glowing

assessment of anyone or anything on the first pass. Henry Willoughby must be more than even she had thought. She boosted him several notches in her esteem.

"I think Ann liked him too," Bunty continued. "She might even consider jurying in some of his paintings for the Guild. What are you chopping?"

Nell was pulling vegetables out of the refrigerator—leeks and celery, fennel and carrot. She added bouquet of fresh thyme, and whoosh of parsley and some sage leaves. Bunty forgot what she was talking about and simply watched Nell begin to construct the turkey soup.

NELL BANE'S POST-THANKSGIVING TURKEY SOUP

> 1 turkey carcass, bones cracked and broken up
> Any pan drippings that haven't been used up in gravy
> Several quarts water and/or chicken stock (preferably homemade)
> 1 bulb fennel
> 2-3 large leeks
> 3-4 carrots
> 3/4 ribs celery
> Parsley
> Olive oil
> Leftover turkey meat, bite-size pieces
> Chopped vegetables (celery, carrot, fennel, leek, parsley)
> Egg noodles

Day 1: Pick as much meat as possible from the turkey carcass. Crack the bones and place in stockpot. Cover with cold water or chicken stock. Bring to boil and skim. Meanwhile prepare the fennel, discarding the feathery fronds; set the stalks aside and quarter the bulb. Chop the leeks, carrots, celery and 1/4 c parsley. When the broth has been skimmed, add the vegetables to the stockpot. Place a pot lid in the stockpot on top of the ingredients to keep the bones submerged, and simmer uncovered the stock for several hours. Cool.*

*Speed cool. Recommended method. Prepare an ice water bath in a roasting pan or dishpan. Lift out as many bones and vegetables as possible. Transfer the stock to a large metal bowl and float the bowl in the ice water bath. When cool, strain the stock and chill overnight.

Day 2: Remove the stock from the refrigerator and lift off accumulated fat. Bring the stock to a simmer; meanwhile chop a new set of vegetables: fennel, leek, celery carrots and parsley.

Heat until the vegetables are tender and have had time to impart their flavor to the soup. Just before serving add egg noodles.

CHAPTER 18

An unfamiliar, hunter-green Jaguar was parked in Willoughby's driveway, and Nell pulled up behind it. She sat for a few moments admiring the car. Hunter-green, she'd decided long ago, was her favorite color of Jaguar.

"Not that I'll ever own one," she murmured but she didn't waste much energy wishing for what she wouldn't have and reached, instead, for the quart of turkey soup she was bringing to Henry Willoughby.

The car was unfamiliar, but the voices inside the house were not. She recognized Henry's voice as she entered the house, and after a moment placed the other as Woodford Stone's. The voices were raised. Nell entered The Shop hesitantly and paused in the doorway until Henry saw her.

"If this is an awkward time," she said, "I can come back later."

Henry waved her in, but she noticed he couldn't—or at least didn't—manage a smile. Stone turned to regard her and his anger seemed to swell. He turned back to Henry.

"Think it over!" he ordered. "I haven't the time to wait forever. And I'll give you a suggestion, Willoughby, I'm not interested in hearing any more of this retired truckle. Your answer better be affirmative unless you want trouble. And this other little caper—this book thing—that'll be trouble too if you don't call it off."

But as he turned to go, Nell spoke up.

"Oh! I'm so sorry, but I think I've blocked you in Mr. Stone. I parked just behind you. So thoughtless. Let me move my car."

And Nell hastily placed the turkey soup on a small table and darted out the door. But as she was opening her car door and preparing to get in, Woodford Stone came running lightly down the two granite slabs that served as Henry's back steps. He moved like a cat and the coiled power in his movement made Nell think of a black panther.

"Mrs. Bane!" he called imperiously. "A moment there!"

Nell waited for Stone's approach and he approached right into her face. Unable to step back without falling into her car, she drew back as far as possible, but Woodford Stone pushed his face a few inches farther right into hers.

"What do you think you're playing at?" he demanded. "What's your little game here?"

Nell was mystified and she stammered, wishing frantically that she could be more controlled—more poised.

"I...I don't know what you mean."

"This book that you think you are writing with Willoughby. Don't you realize how dangerous it is? Do you have any idea— the least freaking clue—about the wheels that book could set in motion? The damage it could do? It would be a juggernaut. A *Gotterdammerung*."

Nell was too confused and overwhelmed to speak, and Stone went right on.

"I just gave Willoughby an ultimatum in there and I'm going to give you one too. Cease and desist. Immediately. Or I won't be responsible for the consequences, but I promise you there will be consequences."

Woodford Stone had apparently finished what he had to say, but he continued to stand with his face inches from hers and a scowl that grew darker with each second. Finally, as if to release her, he stepped back, jangled his automatic key and the Jaguar started with a throat-clearing sound.

Shaking, Nell dropped into the front seat of her own car and scratched the key into the ignition. Her hand was trembling. It took her a moment to think which gear to put the car into, then she backed very slowly down the driveway and pulled onto the verge until Stone's car swept down the drive, paused a moment while its gears were shifted, then accelerated down the road.

Wondering what the consequences might be, Nell made her shaky way back into Henry's house. In The Shop, she noticed that Henry didn't look any more stable than she felt.

"He said something about a *Gotterdammerung*, Henry. What did he mean by that?"

"The destruction created by the gods of all things as they went into the final battle with evil—that's what it means," Henry answered soberly. "Beyond that, I cannot tell."

"Evil," Nell repeated under her breath. "Exactly. But what consequences was he talking about?" she wondered.

But Henry Willoughby couldn't say. Or wouldn't.

A thought popped up in Nell's mind like a flag on a mailbox.

"Henry! He wouldn't blackmail *you* by threatening to do something to me, would he?"

Looking miserable, Henry lifted his shoulders helplessly. Nell was quick to rush her words.

"Henry Willoughby, don't you dare come out of retirement to do one more job for Woodford Stone! I don't like him, Henry. I don't trust him. He is threatening both of us. He's... why he's just a *bully*."

This caused Willoughby to laugh explosively and with his laughter, the dark energy in the room seemed to split open, then evaporate.

"Just watch out for yourself, Nell," he told her, "and I'll watch my step too. And no, I don't intend to accept Woodford's new project. Now tell me, what's in that jar?"

"Post-Thanksgiving turkey soup," Nell told him. "Just the thing for some courage."

CHAPTER 19

Nell was busy watching her back. It was hard to remember to do this though and sometimes she brought herself up short, realizing she'd let her attention lapse. But she and Henry Willoughby continued to meet regularly for their memoir sessions, and as the days went by with no further sign from Woodford Stone and since no calamity befell either of them, Nell's guard relaxed.

Nell wanted to know more about Henry's painting—the ones that had true HHW signatures in the lower right hand corners. Within her curiosity, was an ulterior motive. While she needed to see these paintings for the memoir, she also planned to secretly audition Henry's work for possible inclusion in the new Guild shop.

Willoughby was vague.

"Oh, here and there," he said. "They're around."

Nell pressed. "Where? I want to see some. I want to hear some stories about actual paintings. Great forgeries."

Henry regarded her seriously.

"Very well then, I'll tell you about my masterpiece. My greatest forgery. I'll tell you about Charlotte Amberson."

"I don't remember you mentioning her," Nell said.

"Well, I never met Charlotte," Henry replied. "She died, you see, back in 1889, some years before even *I* was born."

Nell was ready. And so was the Sony recorder, its red light looking serious.

"The ethereal Charlotte Amberson, that's how people spoke of her. She sounded to me like she was a princess in a fairy tale. A real once-upon-a-time fairy tale."

"Tell me the story," Nell begged.

"Well once upon a time—that's the way good stories should start—there was a man named John Amberson. He was a Boston financier and a terribly wealthy man. Frankly I think Amberson was a robber baron of some sort, but never mind that. He was wealthy and he had a daughter named Charlotte whom he adored. She was reputed to be a girl of astonishing beauty. A take-your-breath-away beauty.

"When she was only nineteen, Charlotte Amberson died suddenly. No one is certain why. In those days, fevers and conditions could come on quickly and within days or hours a person—even a young and healthy person—could be dead. Think of the summer fever that was so deadly and so feared in medieval times. Think of the Spanish influenza that took the lives of thousands here in the United States. Or maybe it was just a congenital thing. In those days there was no way of knowing about a leaky heart or the onset of an aneurysm.

"Well the long and short of it was, Charlotte Amberson died, and her poor father was distraught. And he bitterly regretted that he hadn't acted on something that he'd been meaning to do. He had always meant to have Charlotte's portrait painted by none other than John Singer Sargent.

"As they say, though, the road to hell is paved with good

intentions, and intending to have his daughter's portrait painted was no consolation to John Amberson.

Nell waited, spellbound.

Henry Willoughby paused.

"I believe there's some iced tea in the kitchen, my dear. Would you like a glass? I find I'm quite parched."

Nell really didn't want a glass of iced tea. She wanted to hear the rest of the story, but it seemed terribly rude to deny her host and storyteller something to drink when he was parched, so she nodded acceptance, and Henry tootled off to the kitchen.

Established once again in The Shop, Henry took a long pull on the iced tea and pronounced it the very thing.

"Where was I?"

"Explaining that John Amberson never had Charlotte's portrait painted."

"Oh. Yes. Well then. That was that."

Henry Willoughby turned his hands palm up.

"End of story," he said.

"No!" Nell felt fouled. "Not fair. You were building up to a cracking good tale and now...end of story?"

She was incredulous.

Willoughby smiled.

"Well it *was* the end of the story—for a while. Charlotte Amberson was buried in Mount Auburn Cemetery and after a time people stopped saying what a shame it was that she was gone and poor John Amberson and so forth, and then they forgot about her."

Nell wasn't about to let this go. She sat very still. She saw Henry was watching her closely and she smiled.

"Go on," she said quietly.

CHAPTER 20

"The story of Charlotte Amberson had been buried nearly as long as she had, when Woodford Stone disinterred it," explained Henry Willoughby. "Dug up the story, not Charlotte. Maybe Woodford was bored. Maybe he needed a socking influx of cash. Maybe...well, I don't know. But he was nosing around, as he was so good at doing, and somewhere he heard about Charlotte Amberson and her father's grief, and Stone began hatching an elaborate scheme. Of course it involved me."

Nell, sensing they might be approaching the nut of Willoughby's memoir, settled in, prepared to listen.

"To begin with, Stone thought he'd...well...*correct* the historical fact that no portrait existed of Charlotte. In his mind, the correction would be simple. He would appear to find a painting of the deceased girl—a painting by no less an artist than John Singer Sargent. He would make a huge too-doo over the discovery—to whet the appetites of the art community, you know—and then he would sell or auction the painting for a fabulous amount of money."

Somewhere, during this explanation—probably at the mention of Sargent's name—Nell's jaw had dropped in astonishment. Now she tried to speak.

"But how ...? But he just can't... But that makes no make sense... Such a brazen... Hair-brained!" she exclaimed in summary.

During her tirade, Henry Willoughby sat there smiling calmly and nodding his head.

"You are right. Everything you said, or tried to say, is correct."

He beamed.

Nell gave him a shrewd look.

"There's more, isn't there? Okay, give me the whole story."

"For one thing, Woodford needed to get his hands on the painting—a painting that didn't exist and never had existed. Then he'd need to provide provenance—uncontroversial proof that the thing was a real John Singer Sargent work. He'd need to invent the cock-and-bull story of all cock-and-bull stories, yet it would have to be plausible enough for the experts to swallow."

Henry Willoughby was enjoying himself. He sat back in his chair and actually grinned. Nell could have lurched at his neck with her bare hands to get his tale moving. She began to sputter again.

"So you did it?" Her voice scaled higher. "You actually forged a Sargent? And got away with it? *Henry!*"

"Yep," he laughed. "Yes, yes, and yep."

Nell couldn't believe it.

She shook her head to clear it.

"This is going to be a bigger deal memoir than I'd ever imagined," she muttered. "So?"

"In the first place, I told myself that whatever Stone was going to do, wasn't my business. He was going to give me a down payment for creating the painting—however I did it—but it would have to be a highly credible forgery. That's all I'd have to do. I understood that.

"In the second place, it was helpful that nobody knew what Charlotte Amberson had looked like. Well, that was helpful in some ways but it was also a drawback in others. Still, I felt I needed to work from some kind of reference, so I'd have to find one.

"In the third place, I knew I'd have to do intensive research on Sargent's work—on his media and especially on his style. John Singer Sargent had a long career. He is known for his portraits but he also painted landscapes and murals and what are called subject pieces. And his style evolved and changed throughout his career. Every artist's does, I think.

"The window I had to work in was narrow. Dates were critical. Death records showed that Charlotte Amberson died in 1889 at age nineteen. Therefore, Sargent would have painted her around that time and not later. There, we got lucky. Sargent lived and painted in Europe, but he made his first trip to Boston in 1888; then he went home in 1889 returned later that year and stayed through 1890. So it was possible that Charlotte could have sat for him within that span of time. The dates also suggested the style that Sargent typically used around then. My work had to be consistent with the way Sargent was painting at that time."

He looked at Nell and raised his eyebrows.

"Tall order, eh?"

Nell, her eyes wide, could only gulp and nod.

"So I did a little research of my own," Henry continued, "and I was lucky enough to unearth a simple pencil sketch someone had made of Charlotte when she was about nine years old. It was an amateur sketch. A faded little profile. It wasn't much but it was a bit of help suggesting the shape of the face, the eye, so forth. You've seen some of Sargent's portraits, haven't you?"

"Of course," Nell said, "At the Gardner, the MFA and in a dozen art books."

"I'm a good forger," Willoughby said, "but I'm not quite up to the brushwork of a portrait like *Madame X* or *John D. Rockefeller*. But an oil sketch, along the lines of *Vernon Lee* or *Madame Gautreau Drinking a Toast*...well, I'd stand a better chance with those. They are... I guess I'd call them more informal. In *Vernon Lee*, Sargent painted his friend Violet Paget in a single sitting. Perhaps it was just an off-the-cuff idea one afternoon when they were sitting around a drawing room conversing. The pencil work is still visible on the subject's jaw, but the portrait isn't dashed-off or clumsy. It's very sensitive and revealing of character. It's like a living thing. It's a charming portrait. I'd love to own it."

Henry cocked an eyebrow.

"Art people might call the work elliptical; details that the artist chose to leave out worked as much as the brush strokes to capture the essence of his friend—to catch her very vitality."

Henry leaned back in his chair and threw one ankle over the opposite knee. Nell could see him warming to his subject in a way he had never opened up before.

"You know about the shocking Madame X," he said. "In reality, Madame Gautreau was as shocking in the flesh as she was in the portrait. She was known for her lavender face powder that made her skin look like porcelain as well as for her scandalous décolletage."

"Even a barbarian such as I knows about her," Nell smiled.

"That painting just about ruined Sargent's career," Henry said, "and it probably didn't flatter her reputation much either. But around the same time that he painted that infamous portrait—about 1883, I think it was—he also painted her in an oil sketch—oil on wood—to completely different affect. Warm and intimate this portrait is. He softened her with broad brushwork that is highly visible. Very different indeed from the porcelain surface of *Madame X* —a surface that you can't believe a brush even touched. In the sketch, he painted her by lamplight so she seems to emerge from that darkened background as warm and human. As in *Vernon Lee*, the subject in this portrait is mobile. Utterly human."

"So as I began work on *The Ethereal Charlotte Amberson*. I went inside Sargent as he painted in Capri—as he must have painted *Head of Capri Girl*. And I traveled with him back to the River Kennet in 1888 as he painted *A Morning Walk*, letting myself transition a bit into Sargent's Impressionistic phases by admitting a touch of Claude Monet into my brush."

"And all of those young women, those subjects, swirled by me as I painted, and they all left something of themselves in the portrait—the portrait of Charlotte Amberson."

"So you finished it," Nell breathed.

"I did."

"I want to see it." Nell demanded.

"Very well," said Henry Willoughby. "So you shall."

CHAPTER 21

Nell was deeply engrossed in writing Charlotte Amberson's story, but Bunty Whitney and Ann Fitzmaurice had other plans for Nell's time. They were pulling up the socks of The Backstreet Guild of Artists and Craftsmen, preparing to throw open its doors, and needing a brochure.

"You're a writer," Bunty told Nell. "It's easy for you."

Nell protested, but Bunty wasn't listening.

"If you'd just sit down and do it," she said, "instead of thinking up all the reasons you can't, you'd have the brochure done in no time!"

Nell silently conceded that Bunty was probably right, and so she pushed Charlotte Amberson aside and applied her mind to the Guild.

The Guild shop—or gallery as Bunty had begun calling it— was small but it did have good light and ample wall space for the paintings that Ann Fitzmaurice was marshaling from all her artist friends. She was delighted to have scored several sculptures as well, and these would anchor the center of the shop, along with pieces from Bunty and other local potters; these would be displayed on plinths of differing heights and lit attractively from above. There would be two cases where handmade silver jewelry would sparkle, and fiber art could be hung or arranged on tables. Ann was especially pleased with a set of hand-loomed placemats. These she had arranged in an attractive table-scape that featured place settings of Bunty's pottery.

Nell, intending to soak up ambiance, visited the space on one of those blue-sky winter days when the sunlight seems to shoot sparks. The Guild shop shone. Bunty and Ann and several other people were practically twittering as they put finishing touches on the displays and argued gently about where objects should be arranged or hung.

The excitement was contagious, and Nell was eager to get home to her computer where she could expect the brochure copy to practically write itself.

"A job well done," she told herself, pushing away from her laptop several hours later. She glanced at the kitchen clock. It was late and she'd overlooked supper, but there was a pint of vegetable barley soup that could be quickly heated and a stick of ciabatta that could be revived in the oven. Perhaps best of all, there was a program on PBS that she wanted to see. She was all set.

Later that night Nell heard a car door close. It didn't slam, but it was an intentional-sounding close, firm but quiet, as if the person wanted to secure the door without making noise. It sounded close. She waited, but no one approached the house or rang the bell. In the silence, Nell shivered. What was the feeling? She'd had it before. For some reason, Woodford Stone walked into her mind. She felt his energy and she shivered again.

Nell stood up quietly, slipped toward the kitchen door and

turned the lock. She stood for a moment wondering if the front door was secure, then decided it probably was. People rarely came and went through her front entrance. Still, best to be sure. She noticed she was moving through the house with an odd sliding motion as if she were ice skating or trying to shuffle along on small throw rugs.

There was a car in front of the house. Its dark color and its shape, long and low, was all that Nell could make out. Then, with a thump of sightless recognition, she knew.

Crouching, Nell made for the kitchen and phoned Bunty.

"Why are you whispering?" Bunty wanted to know. She had also lowered her voice and was speaking in a guttural growl.

"Because I think there's someone outside," Nell hissed. "An intruder."

"Call the police," Bunty hissed back.

"I can't," whispered Nell.

"Why not?"

"Because they might be busy with something important," Nell whispered. "What if they came and this was nothing and while they were here, something important happened somewhere else in town. A fire or someone having a heart attack or a small child choking..."

"Nell!" Bunty had stopped whispering. "Call the cops immediately or I will!"

Cowed, Nell quietly hung up the phone and dialed 911.

Two Newburyport policemen and Bunty Whitney arrived at the same time. The women explained. The cops listened.

"Take a look around outside Bill," one of them said. "If there was a car here, it was gone when we pulled up. You got your flashlight?"

"'Course," said Bill.

"There were footprints in the snow," Bill reported. "I'd

say a size eleven, maybe twelve, print. Diagonal treads. Only one guy. Prints didn't come up as far as the porch but they're under all the front windows. Looks like maybe you had a peeper, Ms. Bane."

Bill's partner—Nell never did learn his name—wanted to know if Nell had been having any trouble with anyone.

For some reason Nell was embarrassed to admit that she had been threatened, but with Bunty standing an ominous guard, she knew she couldn't get away without admitting it.

Bunty invited herself into the discussion.

"It was a couple weeks ago, wasn't it Nell? A guy named Woodford Stone. He pushed her and told her to stop working on a book she's writing."

"Well, he didn't really push me, Bunty..."

"He did too," Bunty said protectively. "You try to minimize everything..."

"Okay," the chief cop was decisive. "We'll log this, and if you feel threatened again or feel you are being watched, you give us a call immediately, okay?"

Nell tried to explain that she didn't want to bother them because maybe they had important things to attend to, but Bill and Bunty and the second cop all hushed her up.

She hushed.

CHAPTER 22

The portrait of the ethereal Charlotte Amberson wasn't the only thing that had Nell's curiosity stirred. As eager as she was to see the painting, she was also dying to know how Woodford Stone had managed to cobble up certification good enough to dupe the knowledgable and necessarily skeptical art community.

Henry Willoughby feigned insulted surprise when she asked about this.

"Why my dear Nell, after all this time and all this talking, why would you doubt my ability to create documents that appear as the very navel of authenticity?"

Nell had to laugh as she apologized, and Henry laughed along with her.

"So you forged the certification along with the painting?" Nell shook her head. "Henry, you are incorrigible."

Still, Nell wasn't about to let him off the hook.

"But where is the painting? When will I get to see it?" she demanded.

"The painting is in the possession of the Pingree Cabot Museum," he told her. "Woodford Stone kicked up quite a bit of interest in her and so there was a biding battle when she came up for sale. The director at the PCM wanted that painting so badly he could taste it. He thought the museum deserved to have it, and he must have shaken down every patron the museum had in order to raise the money to get it."

Henry looked thoughtful.

"I haven't visited Charlotte in quite a while but the last time I saw her, she was in the gallery that houses the PCM's Americana collection. When would you like to visit? What about a week from today?"

"A week," Nell said. "I guess I can wait a week."

She was silent, trying to imagine Henry's forgery actually hanging in a gallery in the Pingree Cabot Museum.

"And they've never known it wasn't real?" she marveled. "Never suspected?"

Pretending again to be insulted, Willoughby drew himself up to his full five foot three inch height.

"Why my dear, you bruise my ego. I am a professional. I know what I'm doing. For one thing, I am expert at handling edges," Henry said.

Seeing that Nell looked mystified, he explained, "An edge is a place where two shapes or forms meet, or shades of light and dark. There are hard edges and soft ones, and one way to quickly identify a fake, or an amateur work versus a professional, is to look at the edges. If there is a sharp edge between everything, the painting looks like a coloring book—like the artist just stayed in the lines and painted in the colors.

"Now Sargent was a master of edges. He was said to run a rag over his paintings every night to soften all the edges because he believed that the decision of hard edges versus soft shouldn't be made until the artist is nearing the end of the painting.

That's the time to make the decisions between hard and soft. If you're going to credibly forge a Sargent, it's very important to understand this.

"The artist," he continued, "is in the business of destroying so he can create."

Nell humbly absorbed this. But then she had another thought.

"Now tell me now how Woodford Stone pulled off the story of the portrait?"

But Willoughby shook his head.

"I'd prefer to wait and let the copy in the museum's catalog explain that." He twinkled. "Woodford Stone wrote the copy himself."

CHAPTER 23

"What is that smell?" Bunty Whitney wanted to know. Since the nighttime visit from Woodford Stone and the Newburyport police, Bunty had been keeping careful track of Nell.

She kicked Nell's back door shut with her foot and lifted her nose, sniffing like a rabbit scenting danger on the wind.

"Soup."

"Soup? You're kidding—what kind?"

"Sauerkraut."

"Gaaaah! You can't be serious."

Nell sighed. "I couldn't resist. The recipe sounded too fascinating to pass up. My friend Robin says her grandmother used to make it. And right now I'm killing time until Henry and I are ready to do the next installment of his memoir."

ROBIN'S GRANDMA'S SAUERKRAUT SOUP

1/3 cup dried mushrooms reconstituted in 1-1/2 cups boiling water

1 32-oz jar sauerkraut, drained and rinsed
(Save the juice drained from the sauerkraut)
1-1/2 quarts water
1/2 cup barley
5 T butter
1 onion, finely diced
5 T flour
salt and pepper

Steep mushrooms in boiling water until soft, drain and finely chop. Save the mushroom-steeping juice for the soup. Place the sauerkraut, and water in a 5-quart Dutch oven and bring to a boil. Add mushrooms and mushroom juice and simmer for one hour. Rinse barley, add it to pot and simmer until barley is tender. Melt the butter and sauté onions in butter until soft. Add flour to the onions, along with some liquid from the soup, and stir until smooth. Add onions to the soup along with the sauerkraut and sauerkraut juice. Season, as needed with salt and pepper. If the soup is too thick, thin it with the saved sauerkraut juice.

Bunty, having criticized the idea of sauerkraut soup and read the recipe, decided that she owed it to herself to sample some.

"This soup is going to take a while to cook," she said, "and I have a feeling it will be even better tomorrow. Save me a bowlful, will you? These grandma recipes are usually delicious. I'll be back tomorrow to see if that holds true."

CHAPTER 24

The Pingree Cabot Museum was a fusty old curiosity shop when Nell first knew it. Its collections were amalgamations of artifacts connected with sailing days. Bowsprits broken off whaling ships and enormous porcelain jars lugged home as booty from the China Trade. Groups of school children on annual field trips, bemused and goggle-eyed, wandered the dusty galleries, grateful for any excuse to be away from their classrooms for the day. Nell remembered a huge painting by Abbott Thayer that dominated a gallery dedicated to American art—one of his militaristic, but posthumous-looking angels, who seemed to have been posed in death rather than life. From its prominent position, Nell had inferred that the PCM curators had considered it a jewel in their crown.

But several decades ago, the Pingree Cabot had undergone nothing short of a metamorphosis. A huge capital campaign had brought success beyond wildest expectations. A daring young architect had been hired to greatly expand the museum, and the transformation was staggering. Entering the atrium was like stepping into an entire universe encapsulated in glass. Struts and spars four stories above supported a glass ceiling— a vast skylight—and now, when Nell visited, she had an exalted feeling as if she were standing on the bridge of a celestial sailing ship. The architect had referenced the PCM's nautical heritage and created a twenty-first century space where visitors felt inspired and humbled and exalted. The Pingree Cabot Museum had become a destination.

The directors and curators had obviously received a good share of the new money, and they had been busy buying and filling the museum with enviable treasures.

In the company of Henry Willoughby, Nell was visiting. She was glad to push through the doors and into the atrium where it was warm even though the winter temperature pressed on the glass. Henry insisted on paying the admission fees, then took some time to rifle through the museum's brochures before selecting the one for the Americana Collection.

"Come, my dear," he told Nell. "Step this way. There is someone waiting to meet you."

Like most of the permanent collections, the Americana was on the first floor, and double glass doors divided the quiet bustle of the atrium from the dim, almost sacred space of the galleries.

"The museum is justifiably proud of this collection," Nell's guide whispered. "Look at the walls. They only use Farrow & Ball paints on the exhibitions. Took a leaf from the Metropolitan, they did. That's all they'll use at the Met."

Nell obediently observed the walls—an indescribably delicious blue."

"Oval Room Blue," Willoughby said.

"You actually know the name of the paint color?" Nell was amazed.

"Like an old friend," said Henry. "And you must remember

who you're talking with, my dear. I have an eye."

Henry Willoughby appeared to be in no hurry. He ambled through each gallery slowly, stopping now and then to admire or comment on a particular painting.

"The museum's Winslow Homer."

Henry centered himself before the rather modest-size oil of a fishing dory. He nodded to himself and rocked fore and aft on his small feet.

"It was a grand day for the staff when they acquired this," he told Nell. "A Winslow Homer at last. How could they claim to have a decent collection of American art without a Homer?"

Nell thought of the Abbott Thayer and looked around for it. She didn't see it, but perhaps it would show up later. Henry strolled on.

Silver serving pieces—punch bowls and teapots—from Revolutionary War days and lighted like jewelry winked from glass cases. Bowls from Canton tipped invitingly forward to display their interior designs. Oil portraits of Americans looking haughtily into the middle distance, most in three-quarter poses, appeared to be thinking of something far away. What, Nell wondered, were the subjects actually thinking as they sat for their portraits?

And then—and Nell wasn't actually prepared for it—they were in front of *The Ethereal Charlotte Amberson*. A museum light above it supplied the perfect amount of illumination. A modest card pinned to the wall next to the frame introduced her: John Singer Sargent c.1888. 14.2 x 19.3.

The card had no information beyond this, and Henry handed the brochure he'd been carrying to Nell. She took it without seeing it, and continued to stand for some minutes staring at the oil sketch. She couldn't get over it. It was good. No, it was more than good. She hadn't expected...hadn't known...

She realized that Henry was watching her. A small smile kept ticking at the corners of his mouth.

"Henry, I hadn't realized how... how really good this painting could be. It has such life. Charlotte looks like someone you'd like to know. You'd know you'd really like her."

Nell's amazement seemed to delight the elderly man.

"Then I've done my job well."

He giggled.

"The PCM was pleased to get its hands on this baby, I can tell you that. They'd been licking their chops to get a Sargent and they'd missed out on several chances. I'd go so far's to say, they felt they were *entitled* a Sargent. He'd spent a good deal of time here on the North Shore—he'd even been a founder of the North Shore Arts Association—and the PCM looked on him as a homeboy. Well, a Sargent doesn't come available all that often, does it? And the PCM powers-that-be were prepared to pay plenty when the opportunity did come. And now they have it. They have their Sargent."

Nell was suddenly smacked in the face with reality. The Pingree Cabot Museum still didn't have their Sargent. Not really. And they didn't even know that their celebrated acquisition was false. She hardly knew what to say to Henry Willoughby.

CHAPTER 25

Something didn't feel right to Nell. She wasn't sure what it was but there was something—some vibe—coming from Henry that was new, new and disturbing. Something was eating at him. Was he feeling ill? Was he worried? Had he heard something troubling from his sister Muriel over in France?

But no. In fact, Henry denied anything was troubling him. Nothing. Nothing at all.

Nell ventured a wild guess.

"This is just out of left field," she said, fibbing roundly, "but does this have anything to do with Woodford Stone? Is that why he's been around here growling at you?"

Willoughby was vague, but he didn't deny it.

Nell pressed the issue.

"Henry, you've made it plain that you're retired. Is Stone pressuring you?"

Willoughby sighed.

"Well, he is. For one thing, he wants me to pull the plug on the memoir."

Nell was incensed.

"It's your memoir. It has nothing to do with him. How can he make a demand like that?"

"In a sense it does have something to do with him," Henry admitted. "He knows that when the book is published, it will be revealed in black type that my accomplice in my career of crime was none other than Woodford Stone. Of course, I've told him—tried to tell him—that nobody's going to read my modest little memoir. It's going to be the non-event of the decade."

Nell had to admit to herself that she could see reason for Stone's concern.

"But that's still no reason to bully you," she told Henry stoutly.

"Well, I'm afraid there's more to it," he said. "Woodford has come across another *opportunity*—the opportunity of a lifetime, he claims. It has all the elements to entice a man who plays Woodford's game. Someone like Stone would be completely unable to let it slip through his fingers. He could no more turn his back on this deal than an addict can turn away from a drug. His ability to get into the game, though, depends upon one thing. Someone like me."

Henry sighed.

Nell was enraged.

"You can't let him use you like that!" she sputtered. "Tell him...tell him to...."

But then curiosity got the better of her.

"What is the scheme he's proposing?"

Henry sighed again.

"Woodford has fallen in league with a fellow inside the Chrysalis Museum in upstate New York. They have an impressive collection, especially for a small museum that isn't all that well known. Not a large collection perhaps, but one that's worth millions, and one that has an enviable Klee. Something along the lines of *Static Gradation,* I'm told.

"This insider has had business dealings with Stone in the past, and he's approached him again. As Stone tells it, the individual has identified a potential buyer who is willing to pay twenty-million for the Klee. Furthermore, he claims that he is in a position to spirit the painting out of the museum and hang a forgery in its place with nobody being the wiser. Stone uses his connections to get the forgery done and have the authentication faked. Then the employee at the Chrysalis will seamlessly make the swap, then they'll sell the Klee, and split the cash."

"Three ways?" Nell asked. She heard the bitterness in her own tone.

"Except the three shares won't be equal," Henry said tiredly. "They never are."

"You're not going in on this are you?"

"I've told you and I've told Stone that I am retired. I am holding to that."

"I didn't think you could do that modern stuff anyway," Nell told him.

"I said it doesn't interest me," Henry said, "I didn't say I couldn't do it."

He sighed again.

"Oh, there might have been a time I would have gone along with the scheme. A time when I was younger, when the money meant more, when the thrill and the challenge proved too appealing to turn my back. But not now. I'm an old man. I'm through. But Woodford...he can't turn his back. Not on this. It is too enticing."

"But *Woodford* doesn't have to do the work," Nell pointed out in exasperation,

"True," Henry admitted, "but he can badger me and

intimidate and try to manipulate me into dipping my brushes once again."

"And blackmail you?" Nell asked. "Can he do that? Is he doing that?"

But Henry Willoughby wouldn't say.

"I may be retired, but Stone isn't."

"Well, it sounds awfully risky to me."

"Risky? Of course, it's risky. The whole forgery game is about risk. That's part of the reason people like Stone are in it. They love the money and they crave the adrenalin rush that comes with the risk."

"It also sounds incredible to me," Nell said. "Incredible that someone actually is willing to pay twenty million for the painting as well known as this Klee. Why does he want it? What can he do with it? You can't just sell it across the counter like a bag of donuts."

"Who knows why," Henry sighed. "Maybe he'll resell it on the black market. Maybe he has a buyer willing to pay *thirty* million. Maybe he plans to put it in storage for years until the forgery is discovered. Maybe he just wants to hang it in his bathroom and view it from the bathtub."

CHAPTER 26

When confused or overwhelmed, Nell often took solace in Robert Hutchins's company. She made her way into Boston and after circling several times, even scored a parking space on Beacon Hill. The elegant townhouse that Robert shared with Jerry Grasso was restorative simply in its tranquility, and Robert's clarity had a way of centering Nell and resetting her compass.

"You're my compass rose, Robert," she said.

"Well, Nell, I am uncomfortable with the metaphor but I'll overlook it considering your intention is meant to flatter. What's got you in turmoil now? The Henry Willoughby affair?"

Nell admitted it.

"The thing is, Robert, I saw the portrait. The forged Sargent that Henry painted. It's called *The Ethereal Charlotte Amberson*, and Robert, it's good. Better than just good. It *is* ethereal. I went to the Pingree Cabot with Henry and I could hardly believe what I was seeing. Of course I'm no expert, but I can see how the experts at the museum were easily be induced to buy it."

Robert nodded. He cleared his throat.

"Nell, you've been working on this project since last summer and you must be nearing the end. The memoir's almost finished, is it?"

Nell acknowledged that it was.

"Well, then," Robert continued, "you've had plenty of time to get—how shall I put it?—*squidgy* over the forgery business. Why did you wait till now?"

The question was a good one. Nell had to admit that to herself as she thought.

"I don't know...until I saw the painting...saw it actually hanging there in the museum with a card like all the other paintings had and saw the description in the printed brochure and all, it didn't seem...well, real to me."

She frowned.

"Then it hit me. I felt like an invisible fist had pounded on my chest. The Pingree Cabot people believe they own an actual John Singer Sargent—and they don't."

"Ah. Now the ethical aspect rears its head."

Nell nodded glumly.

"I wondered when it would," Robert Hutchins said. "You do realize, Nell, that your Mr. Willoughby is a criminal."

Nell was instantly defensive.

"Henry Willoughby wouldn't hurt a fly. He has killed no one nor beaten anyone nor bilked them out of their life savings. He has never been arrested for so much as jaywalking. Nor has he been charged nor incarcerated for larceny. He is an exemplary citizen with a completely clear record."

Robert dropped his chin, the better to examine Nell from under his eyebrows.

"Willoughby has had the wit—or the simple luck—not to get caught," Robert replied drily. "But he operates outside the law."

"Well, it is all beside the point now," Nell said tartly. "Henry Willoughby is retired. He may be a forger but that is in the past. All he does now are calligraphed Christmas cards and wedding invitations."

Robert Hutchins simply aimed a level look at Nell, never altering his gaze until she, in some discomfort, looked away. Until quite recently, Nell hadn't allowed herself to consider the actual criminal implications of fraud. She supposed she always realized it but she hadn't allowed herself to really believe it, and she was quite defensive, thinking of a number of reasons why Henry's transgressions didn't really count. But once you know something, you can't unknow it, and Nell Bane, who had always trod the moral high road, found herself teetering on a dilemma. And was she implicating herself by joining the deception?

Robert Hutchins suddenly smiled. And to Nell, his smile made things better again.

"Come on," he told her consolingly. "Let's walk around the corner to Beacon Street, and I'll take to you lunch at Mooo. They have an excellent potato and leek soup, and I think the pork belly will restore your soul."

CHAPTER 27

"You promised to tell me Stone's part in the Sargent swindle," Nell said to Henry Willoughby. "I've been dying to hear how he confabulated a story believable enough to wash with the buyers, and it's time you stopped teasing me with it."

"Very well, my dear," Willoughby said agreeably. "In the words of Hamlet's father's ghost, *I shall a tale unfold...*

"So, as I was preparing to paint the portrait of Charlotte—doing research and so forth—Stone, at the same time, was inventing the provenance for the little darling. This is what he claimed...

"He—Woodford Stone—was innocently passing through Rowley Massachusetts one day when he happened upon an estate sale in an old house. It didn't look promising. The house had been vacant for several years after the last resident—a man called Kimball—had died while eating supper at the kitchen table. I believe Woodford said he'd been eating oyster stew. Woodford always liked to tuck in little details like that. Made things more credible, he said. Also it distracted the listeners and drew them off-track. The house, as Woodford described it, wasn't in good shape and hadn't been for a long while before the imaginary Mr. Kimball ate that oyster stew in the kitchen.

"So to get back on track.... There was a whale of a lot of clobber in the house, according to Woodford. The imaginary Kimball had been something of a hoarder, and the condition of the place discouraged even the folks who make a practice of scrounging around estate sales and auctions. Probably smelled bad. You know, that wet plaster-and-lath smell mixed with...well, with whatever. Business that day was kind of slow and the people who were running the sale were thinking about packing it up and calling in the junkers to haul most of the stuff away.

"Woodford, however, with his expert eye, decided to do a pass through the place, and upstairs in a back bedroom, he spied the oil sketch. It looked like it could be a Sargent, he thought, but he wasn't sure. It was filthy, for one thing. It had been in that bedroom since the lady whose chamber it had been cashed in her chips. That lady would have been one Molly Kimball.

"Anyhow, Woodford bought the portrait for fifty dollars. He said it was more than the auction people made all day. And away he went with his prize.

"His research—*alleged* research—showed that Molly Kimball, poor soul and the owner of the painting, was a widow of a late Kimball cousin, but before her name was Kimball, it was Amberson. Molly Amberson. So you know where this is going, don't you?"

Willoughby peered at Nell.

"I have an idea," she answered drily.

"How she'd come to own the oil sketch was anybody's guess—it really doesn't matter— the name lent credibility.

"So Woodford owned the oil sketch by virtue of that fifty

dollars, and he had a scrap of paper from All State Auctions to serve as the bill of sale. And that was his story—the story he fabricated and the story he'd tell over and over.

"The next thing he had to do, though, was prove that the painting was a true work of John Singer Sargent."

Willoughby shot Nell a sharp look.

"You are keeping this straight, aren't you? You aren't being sucked in by the story?"

Nell gave herself a small mental shake the way she'd shake out a dusty little rug. She had, actually, begun to visualize the wretched old house in Rowley—its paint long worn away, the cedar shakes bleached and the porch floor boards sagging. She could smell the old house odor and see the back bedroom where poor Molly Amberson Kimball had spend her last years.

"No," she told Henry guiltily. "I'm with you."

"A good forger is a great artist," Henry continued. "I had to pull stiff, resistant canvas from the late 1800s onto stretchers and even the fasteners had to be old and rusty. Paints had to be absolutely authentic, and since the portrait was said to have hung in that back bedroom for years, it had to show appropriate wear and filth. Molly wasn't great shakes as a housekeeper. It would have been subjected to sunlight, so there would be fading as well as filth. I dirtied up my paints and rusted the fasteners on the stretchers and rubbed wear onto the corners. We got hold of an old frame that had bits of plaster chipping off and we chipped off some more, then we filthied that up as well.

"The risky part—well, one of the riskier parts anyhow—would come when the new owners took the painting apart to clean it. During this kind of exposure many a forgery has been revealed."

"Were you nervous?' Nell wanted to know.

Henry shrugged.

"Oh yes, but probably not as shivery as Stone. His

professional credibility was really on the line."

Henry was ready to continue his story.

"When we had the oil sketch all souped up and ready to go, Woodford allowed his cock-and-bull story to go into the art press. You wouldn't have heard about it in *The Boston Globe,* my dear, but the discovery of an unknown John Singer Sargent oil sketch made headlines in the publications that went into every museum, and every university collection and gallery. Everyone was talking about *The Ethereal Charlotte Amberson.* The chatter went on for weeks.

"Meanwhile, Stone just sat back in Boston with his feet up and a fine cigar burning and waited.

"A number of museums were interested—it was shaping up to be quite a bidding war—but the director at the Pingree Cabot was most keen. The PCM wanted a Sargent so bad they were salivating. They felt they deserved it. Felt they owed it to their patrons and to everybody in the area to have a Sargent in their Americana Collection. After all, here they were, an old New England institution, not some fly-by-night gallery in Albuquerque. They *deserved* to own *The Ethereal Charlotte Amberson.* In their minds, the painting was already theirs. And in the end, they got it.

CHAPTER 28

The day matched Nell's mood. Gloomy. Even the atrium in the Pingree Cabot Museum seemed overcast. Nell paid her admission fee and stepped deeper into the atrium. She wasn't exactly certain why she had come.

Following arrows that pointed upstairs, Nell wandered toward a gallery promising a new show of Caribbean art. She strolled obediently through the exhibition, although it baffled her. She examined the painted walls, wondering which Farrow & Ball paint color she was seeing.

Unmoved and unchanged—and wasn't one supposed to be at least changed if not uplifted by art?—Nell left the Caribbean gallery. Wandering on, she found herself outside the executive offices of the PCM's staff. She was a reader and so she carefully read the small, efficient signs beside each door. Executive Director: Edward Glendenning, she read. Curator, Americana Collection: Elizabeth Beaman.

Nell paused, thinking. Then, taking a pen and small notebook from her bag, she jotted down these names.

"You never know," she told herself.

With a sigh, Nell retraced her steps and returned to the atrium. From there, she turned right and pulled open the doors of the Americana Collection. On this trip, though, she walked straight through the first three galleries to the one where *The Ethereal Charlotte Amberson* lived.

On this uninspired Thursday morning, the museum was all but silent. Apart from an older couple murmuring to each in hushed tones, Nell was alone in the gallery. The couple murmured out and Nell stepped up to face Charlotte Amberson. She stood for a long time.

"What do you think of our Sargent?" asked a pleasant voice just behind her left shoulder.

Nell turned. The voice's owner was as pleasant to look at as she sounded. She appeared to be in her early thirties. Chestnut hair in soft waves fell to her shoulders and her pale gray business suit was perfectly tailored. A lanyard with a photo I.D. hung about her neck.

"I... it's...well, I think it's lovely," Nell said weakly.

If the woman was disappointed in the limp answer, she didn't show it. Instead she gazed at the portrait herself.

"We were fortunate to get it," she said finally. "There were a half dozen serious contenders lusting after it."

So this woman wasn't just some gallery-goer; she was with the PCM. Nell squinted sideways, trying to make out the name on the I.D.

The woman perceptively, put out her hand and admitted with a smile, "I'm with the museum. Elizabeth Beaman."

Nell was struck.

"You're the curator of the Americana Collection," she informed this woman. "Please forgive me for staring. It's just that I imagined a curator would look more like a funeral director."

"Complete with a rusty morning coat and a *pince-nez?*" Elizabeth Beaman laughed.

"Something like that," Nell laughed too.

Side by side Nell and the curator regarded the oil sketch of Charlotte Amberson. Nell couldn't tell what her companion was thinking, but she herself was wrestling with her conscience. Should she reveal to Elizabeth Beaman that the museum's prize Sargent was a forgery? Should she, standing there in the gallery with no art credentials whatsoever, confess what she knew?

Nell turned slowly toward Elizabeth Beaman and cleared her throat.

"I was wondering," she said slowly, "about the Abbott Thayer painting. I didn't see it in the galleries."

Elizabeth Beaman smiled.

"Ah. Yes. It's in storage actually. We have far too many pieces to display all at once so... I'm sorry to say, the Thayer didn't make the cut. Frankly, its sentimentality is out of vogue at present. Is it a favorite of yours?"

She seemed amused.

Nell was quick to disassociate herself from the expired-looking angel.

"No," she admitted. "It isn't. I just wondered about it that's all."

Unsure whether to be disappointed in herself or not, Nell sighed. The time had, for a moment, seemed ripe. Today just wasn't the day.

CHAPTER 29

The draft of Henry Willoughby's memoir—*My Place in the Gallery of Rogues*—was complete. Nell held the neatly printed pages in her hands and tapped the sheets on the counter to align them. She had been through several drafts, not to mention a number of edits and rewrites. The draft needed a final proofreading and then it would be ready to place in Henry's hands for what Nell hoped would be his blessing. And with the blessing would come the second of the three payments of Nell's fee.

It had been several weeks since she had seen Henry, and therefore several weeks since their visit to the Pingree Cabot to see the oil sketch of Charlotte Amberson. Nell had been busy though, busy finishing up the memoir and busy helping Ann and Bunty get the Guild shop ready to open. Then Henry, as he'd told her over the phone, had come down with bronchitis, and he wouldn't allow her near the manse. No, not even with chicken soup. It simply wouldn't do for Nell to catch this bug.

Nell worried though. Henry was the age of those elderly people they're always warning you about on the news. The ones who are supposed to get flu shots and now pneumonia shots because their immune systems are said to be frail and compromised. What if he were this close to seeing his memoir in print and then were robbed of the pleasure?

At last, though, on a day that was still cold but a day with enough sun to make Nell believe that somewhere it might be spring, she drove the manuscript to Newbury. It rode on the front seat beside her like a valued passenger.

Henry's driveway was a mess. Snow from careless plowings earlier in the season had frozen in ice clumps along the edges of the drive, while in the center, the snow had melted into the gravel, then frozen again, but now, in today's insistent sunshine, it was on the melt again.

Nell made her way carefully to the house.

Henry Willoughby took a long time to come to the door. When he did come, Nell gasped.

"Henry! Who hit you?"

"Come in, my dear. No one hit me."

"Did you fall? That driveway is a mine field, Henry, you have to be careful..."

But Henry Willoughby was shaking his head and trying to wave off her clucking.

"Slipped in the bathtub is all. Nothing, not a thing to be concerned about."

But Nell didn't agree. One of Henry's eyes was black and there was a contusion on his cheek that featured all the colors on one of his paint palettes, and he was limping.

"I brought the manuscript," Nell said triumphantly, holding it high as proof.

Willoughby took it listlessly. There wasn't a sign of his usual twinkle and Nell's concern reignited. She had an ominous thought. It arrived on a draft of negative energy that seemed to have blown into the room.

"I just wondered, Henry," Nell was aiming for a casual oh-by-the-way tone, "wondered if you'd seen or heard anything lately from Woodford Stone."

The look Henry shot at Nell shocked her. It was at once sharp and furtive. There was suspicion and something else—guilt.

"Stone?" he repeated. "Why, no."

"Henry Willoughby, you are a terrible liar—even for a forger! Tell me."

He sighed.

"Woodford did drop in," he said. "Didn't stay long. Was on his way somewhere else he said."

Nell was disgusted.

"He didn't just 'drop in'," she said sarcastically. "He'd have to make a very intentional effort to come all the way up here from Boston. That's not dropping in. What did he want?"

Henry's shoulders slumped and he looked exhausted. "Oh the usual thing. Nothing to worry about."

Nell had the final question ready.

"Henry. Are those bruises some of his work?"

CHAPTER 30

"Assaulted an old man!" Nell told Bunty hotly. "I tried to get Henry to report it to the Newbury police but he was stubborn."

"There's a lot of that going around," Bunty remarked drily.

"Stone *threatened* Henry," Nell went on indignantly, "and then apparently, roughed him up. Shoved him, and I guess Henry's old knees buckled. I couldn't make out whether the bruises happened in the fall or whether they were from Stone's knuckles."

She signed.

"Anyhow, I think he's going to recover, but I'll keep checking on him."

"Yes, and who's going to check on you?" Bunty demanded.

"Ooopf!" said Nell dismissively. "I'll be okay. I'm not afraid of Woodford Stone."

"Not in daylight, you aren't," Bunty pointed out. "That night a couple weeks ago you weren't so brave."

"I'll take my chances." Nell's tone was lofty.

She got her chance the following Wednesday.

Nell wasn't entirely surprised to run into Woodford Stone again, but she wasn't prepared to encounter him on the streets of Newburyport. She quickly realized the encounter wasn't by chance. He had been waiting for her.

"Lurking, perhaps, Mr. Stone?" she asked, adopting an arch tone in an attempt to cover up a sudden acceleration of adrenaline.

"Slumming," he answered. The anthracite eyes were as opaque as ever.

They stood on the sidewalk as at a stand-off, but it was Stone whose affect melted first.

"Look," he said. His tone was almost reasonable. "I've got something to say to you and I don't want to talk here on the street. Is there a pub or someplace?"

Nell was silent. She certainly didn't want to socialize with Woodford Stone but it did seem fair to hear what he wanted to say, and, after all, she couldn't be sure that it was Stone who had visited her that night. She relented. "The Grog. It's just over on Middle Street. Not far."

She began walking. Stone fell in beside her but as the pair marched down State Street, a passerby would not have described them as a couple—or even as two people who knew one and other. Nell was determined to keep an impassive expression as well as her distance and apparently Stone felt the same.

At The Grog, he reached for the handle and held the door for her. Nell nodded curt thanks, and the darkness of the popular Newburyport pub swallowed them.

The aroma of years of beer consumption closed over Nell. They paused, letting their eyes adjust to the darkness, then made their way to a table against a wall.

"Sam Adams," Nell said flatly without waiting for the waitress's pleasantries or her request to take their order. She lifted her chin defiantly.

"Same," said Stone.

Nell folded her hands on the table like a small child just learning to say its prayers. She was determined not to initiate conversation or to try, as she usually did, to put her companion at ease. She was silent. She was grateful though when the waitress returned quickly with the beers. Now she had something to do with her hands. Lift the glass. Sip. Put the glass down. Wipe the wet rings off the tabletop with the little paper napkin.

She waited some more.

Looking unhappy (Nell was pleased to see his discomfort), Woodford Stone also sipped and replaced his glass.

"Look," he said, "we need to talk about the book you are writing for Willoughby."

"Why?"

"Because it could be harmful to him."

Nell cocked her head.

"Oh? How so?"

"If his...ah... transgressions should come to light what do you imagine could happen? Arrest?" he offered with an arched eyebrow. "Incarceration?"

"I think he's quite prepared for anything like that", Nell said.

"You're taking a very exalted road, Mrs. Bane. Pretending to have the wellbeing of your client at heart, when actually you are leading him, like a lamb to slaughter, through the publication of this silly little book. A book, may I add, from which you will derive considerable monetary benefit."

"Henry's memoir isn't going to make me rich or famous," Nell said crisply. "It probably won't make Henry rich or famous either, but he's not writing a memoir to gain either of those things. And he's not writing a silly little book."

"Indeed?" Stone's smirk of disbelief was intended to insult.

"Henry Willoughby has retired, Mr. Stone. And he wants this memoir written and published. He has thought about it, he fully understands what might happen, and he still wants it very much. Enough to pay a healthy amount of money to see it done. Moreover, he's, what? Eighty-six? Eighty-seven now? I don't think he actually cares about being caught."

Stone baited her. "It seems to me that you are pushing him into capture."

Nell looked at him with narrowing eyes.

"It's not Henry you're worried about, is it?" she said perceptively. "It's you. I don't think you care one whit what happens to Henry Willoughby. I think you're worried for your own neck. You're afraid of what will happen to *you* when Henry's memoir is published."

Stone shook his head disgustedly.

"You have quite a chip on your shoulder, Mrs. Bane."

"You are projecting, Mr. Stone."

She thought fleetingly of Bunty and wondered if she would be proud of the way she, Nell, had produced the psychological term. But emboldened—was it the beer?—Nell persevered.

"You spoke of consequences if we went ahead with this book. I suppose *you* would be one of the consequences?"

"I could do a lot of damage," Stone said reflectively. He regarded the beer in his glass in an offhand way. "Damage to Willoughby and damage to you. Damage that you probably can't even conceive of."

Nell grew angry.

"You leave Henry Willoughby alone!" she said fiercely. "Don't you lay a hand on him again. He's an old man and on a physical basis, he's no match for you. But on fair turf, Henry can handle whatever comes. And I'll be standing by him!"

This inspired a derisive snort from Woodford Stone.

Nell pushed back her chair and stood. She aimed a fierce look at him, but he met her stare with a controlled but smoldering look that exceeded hers. As she stamped toward the door, she imagined she smelled brimstone.

Outside, under The Grog's green-and-white striped awnings, Nell had to stand for several moments to regain her equilibrium. She noticed she was still clutching the damp wad of cocktail napkin. She stuffed it into her bag, then, before Stone could emerge from The Grog, she turned and hurried toward State Street. Beyond waited the Guild shop and the solace Bunty Whitney would surely offer. It was only mid-afternoon and her mouth tasted of beer.

CHAPTER 31

Jerry Gasso had announced his intention to visit the Backstreet Guild of Artists and Craftsmen.

"With Jerry, everything's a production," Nell reminded Ann Fitzmaurice and Bunty Whitney, "so brace yourselves."

But Ann and Bunty knew Jerry and loved him for his spontaneity and generosity as well as for his noisy good humor. Besides, as a much in-demand Boston designer, Jerry's patronage and influence could be beneficial to the Guild's business.

There was a party air in the shop when Jerry, carrying two shopping bags, burst in with Nell Bane in his wake. Three customers perusing pottery and silver jewelry, turned to see the source of the cheerful disruption.

"Ladies!" cried Jerry. "Show me your wares! Dazzle me! For I have come from far Boston to attend your bazaar."

With Jerry between them, and both vying for his attention, Bunty and Ann guided Jerry through a tour. He insisted on looking at everything. He put on half glasses for minute inspections. He turned items over to study signatures and marks on bottoms. He held blown glass up to the light and held hard-milled soaps to his nose, inhaling each scent.

"Lavender—always a favorite. Sandalwood—of course. Heaven!—basil—never imagined it. Ah ha! Patchouli."

He addressed Bunty, "Takes you right back to your hippie days, doesn't it, Darling?"

"But Ann! This little still life is a perfect pet. Is the artist local? Amazing. But I want to see some of your work. Direct me to a Fitzmaurice immediately."

Suddenly Jerry remembered his shopping bags and from them whipped out two bottles of Moet Chandon.

"A celebration toast!" he cried, as he made coming together sweeping gestures to the customers, "Come! Come everyone! We're drinking to the success of Backstreet Guild and to the health and prosperity of all of you who shop in her."

Before leaving the shop, Jerry had made the cash register ring madly.

"Well it would have rung madly," as Bunty put it, "if we had a cash register. As it was, though, we ran Jerry's card through the credit thing to a tune north of three hundred dollars."

With promises to come back and to bring some clients from Boston, whom Jerry claimed would be mad for this stuff, and with Nell carrying some of his purchase, Jerry Gasso exited the Guild and headed home to Beacon Hill.

CHAPTER 32

Henry Willoughby was delighted.

"But why is it called *cockamamie* cock-a-leekie, Nell?"

"Well, Henry, I don't think any true Scotsman would make this soup with prunes, do you?"

"Good god, woman, you can't be serious!"

But Nell was, and she presented a quart of it to Henry with a grin and a shrug.

"See for yourself," she said. "Like it not. But I'm here so we can work, I believe. You said you had some changes and additions to the memoir? Tell me first, though, did you like the draft?"

Henry did. And Nell observed that his twinkle had nearly returned. She didn't like his color though. Still gray instead of the rosy glow that his cheeks had sported when they first met.

"I thought of a story that should be included in the memoir," Henry said. "I don't know how it slipped my mind, but I would have been very disappointed to have overlooked it."

"Wait till I get the Sony fired up," Nell told him, "Then I'll be all set."

"Well, it happened years ago," Henry began. "At Pleisher's. Some well-heeled folks—I won't tell you the name because you'd recognize it right off. Old family in Boston. A lot of influence. Anyway, they'd come in with a big oil painting that needed restoration. The whole fam-damily, as we used to say, was in that portrait. It needed cleaning and some small repairs and so forth. That was no problem—a little time-consuming, but straight-forward work—and Uncle Milty set me to work on it."

He chuckled, remembering.

"So I'd put in quite a bit of time, in between other jobs, of course. Pleisher didn't turn things around on a dime, you understand. Part of the delay, I used to think, was theater, but anyway a month or two had gone by when into the shop comes someone from the family. They'd decided that they wanted one of the family members removed from the portrait. Painted out. I can't remember why just now—can't remember what the fellow had done, if indeed I'd ever known—but they insisted. Pleisher resisted. Tried to talk them out of it because the fellow was very prominent in the portrait. If we painted him out, which we could certainly do, there remained the problem of a big awkward space where his head had been."

Nell was fascinated. She wondered who this family was and her imagination began auditioning candidates.

"In the end, the family won the tussle with Pleisher, and he came to me and we figured out a work-around."

"What?" Nell wanted to know.

"We worked out that the family had a dog—a big dog fortunately. An Irish setter. And after I'd eliminated the miscreant, I over-painted him with the setter. I sat the beast right up in the middle of the family group just as proud and prominent as you please."

When the family came in to claim the portrait, everyone held their breath. Gomes, Cynthia what's-her-name, me. Well, old Milton Pleisher," Henry shook his head, "he unveiled the painting as if it's a Rembrandt or something and they loved it. The family thought it was brilliant. Then Pleisher, who never left a dime on the table, told them that his original estimate was out the window and he threw out a new number that would have singed the eyebrows of most people, but these folks never turned a hair. Just opened the checkbook and toddled off with their family portrait."

"You're not going to tell me who they were, are you," Nell said.

"It wouldn't be good for you to know," Henry told her soothingly.

He lapsed into thought.

"Today now, today that wouldn't be a problem. People wouldn't even understand the issue. PhotoShop solves everything today."

COCKAMAMIE COCK-A-LEEKIE

    2 large chicken quarters
    5 c chicken stock
    Bouquet garni
    1 lb. leeks
    12 prunes soaked in water 1 hour
    salt and pepper to taste
Oaty dumplings
    3/4 regular oats
    1 c whole-wheat bread crumbs
    1 T fresh herbs, chopped
    salt/pepper

1/4 c butter

2-3 T cold water.

In a large saucepan, place chicken breasts, the stock and bouquet garni. Bring to boil, then simmer 30 minutes. Remove the chicken and cool the stock. Remove the bouquet garni and skim off any fat from the surface of the soup. Trim the leeks and cut them lengthwise. Wash them thoroughly, then cut then into 1-inch pieces. Add the leeks and prunes to soup. Simmer 25 minutes. Cut the cooled chicken into small pieces and add to soup. Season with salt and pepper.

To make the oaty dumplings: combine the oats and bread crumbs in a medium-sized bowl. Cut in the butter. Add cold water and mix into a dough. Shape into small balls and drop into soup. Cover and simmer 15 minutes.

CHAPTER 33

Nell had the inescapable feeling of being watched. Well, that was alright because she was watching too. She found excuses to call Henry, thought up questions to ask him or to verify details in the changes he'd wished to make in the manuscript. Henry assured her that he was fine, fine. And Nell put her laptop on the kitchen counter and worked her way through the manuscript again, editing as she went.

At her back she always seemed to feel a presence. But the presence was silent, and since she'd parted with Woodford Stone inside The Grog, Nell hadn't seen a sign of him. She blamed her overactive imagination.

A Newburyport patrol car rolled slowly down Nell's quiet street and she thought she recognized Bill's face. Had Bunty alerted them?

The ominous sense persisted. She sought Robert's advice.

"What do you think Stone could do, Robert? Is there any way he could sabotage the memoir?"

"Short of hacking your computer or stealing your laptop,"

Robert said, "or implicating himself, which I very much doubt he'll do, I don't see there's much he can do."

But Nell, feeling paranoid, put Henry's files on two thumb drives and stashed them safely in a pottery soup tureen in Bunty Whitney's studio. It was an especially pretty tureen Nell thought, glazed with soft greens and blues.

At night, dreams—actually nightmares—twisted Nell's bed sheets into ropes and frayed her sleep. Woodford Stone cavorted through her subconscious, darting here and there through a landscape that seemed to be connecting galleries in the Pingree Cabot Museum—galleries that swam and changed and morphed into other galleries. Walls expanded and contracted like fun house mirrors. Caribbean art came alive and leaped from the walls.

In the morning, exhausted, Nell lay still and tried to organize the elements of nocturnal torment. She had a neat mind. She knew she could establish order. But this would take an energy she did not feel this morning.

On one hand, there was Woodford Stone. She might need to mount a defense against his planned consequence. But since she didn't know what he had planned, this was almost impossible. So she watched. And despised the feeling that she was being watched. She felt intimidated.

On the other hand, the ethical issue of the forged Charlotte Amberson hanging in the PCM pressed heavily upon her, and that was something she could act upon. One option would take her to the offices of Elizabeth Beaman and the museum director, Edward Glendenning where she would calmly explain that *The Ethereal Charlotte Amberson* was a forgery.

She imagined herself sitting there. At first they wouldn't believe her. They would demand to know how she could make that assertion. Nell would explain about Henry Willoughby and Woodford Stone and eventually the whole story would be revealed. But what would happen then?

Nell's lively imagination capered out of control and she saw a net, like a fishing net, flung over the hapless head of H. H. Willoughby. He was publically humiliated, made to stand trial. Nell created a trial that drew crowds on the order of Marathon day in Boston with the media jostling and microphones being shoved and ...

Could she do that to Henry? How could she betray that dear, elflike man who had come to be so much more than a client? He had become a dear friend and one of whom she felt terribly protective.

To reveal or remain silent? There were two opposing ethical situations here and neither choice offered any reward or peace of mind. To whom did Nell owe allegiance?

"Two roads diverged in a yellow wood," she murmured. But rather than choosing one over the other, she dithered there at the crossing, unable to put her foot on either path.

CHAPTER 34

In The Midwest Museum of Modern Art, located improbably in Perrysburg, Ohio, director Anthony Doheny made a horrifying discovery. The museum's Jackson Pollock was a fake.

Nell learned about this from Henry Willoughby. In retirement, Henry still maintained a lively interest in the art scene and was still attuned to knowledgable sources, and he remained on the subscription lists of a number of publications.

"How did they find this out?" she asked Henry.

"Car paint," Henry chuckled. "It must have been a very clumsy forgery indeed. The forger used automobile paint and it started peeling off. A really professional forger researches materials and is careful to use pigments consistent with the period. Apparently, in the MMMA case, the paint began coming off while the alleged Pollock was hanging right on the gallery wall. And it sounds like the MMMA didn't do due diligence."

Willoughby chuckled again. He was having a good time.

"Chevrolet blue. Ferrari red." Henry giggled. "I can only imagine it."

"Of course," he continued. "It isn't all that hard to forge a Pollock. Or a Rothko for that matter. Just stretch a giant canvas—or even use sheetrock—and fling some paint at it. Smear it around or just let it drip like water in a car wash. But there's a caveat!" Henry held up a warning finger, "the materials have to be authentic."

Nell was fascinated.

"So what's going to happen now?" she wanted to know.

"It's anybody's guess," Henry told her, "although I know two things that will happen. First this Doheny fellow will comb back through the museum's records and receipts to find out how they came upon this painting. And when they know where it came from and who authenticated it, they will put the word out to museums and universities and galleries all over the country to announce the forgery and expose the certifier. What legal actions the MMMA takes—if any—remain to be seen."

"Might they go after the actual forger as well as the certifier?" Nell asked timidly.

"They might." Henry shrugged. "Who knows?"

He chuckled again.

"But stand by. This could be interesting."

"Henry," she said, "you never forged a Pollock, did you?"

The question disgusted Willoughby.

"I never messed around with those modernists," he said dismissively. "They didn't interest me. Where is the challenge in what they do, I ask you? To me, it's like the story of the king's new clothes—everyone ooh-ing and aah-ing and making a big fuss over something they don't understand. Something that someone else tells them is art. Sheep! That's what most of those collectors are."

He stopped abruptly and held up the warning finger again.

"Mind you! Mind you, now! Some modern stuff is genius. I even include some Pollock in the bunch, but a lot of it is rot, and it's easy to fake rot."

But Nell, for some reason, felt a frisson of fear crawl up her neck.

CHAPTER 35

A new worm of a concern—just a thought, really—one that had lived half-dormant in Nell's mind, was squirming its way toward the surface and coming closer to her consciousness. It was a matter to bring to Bunty Whitney. Nell knew Bunty would be annoyed. And she was.

"I need some help with a psychological thing," Nell said.

"Then find a psychotherapist. I'm a potter."

"Oh come on, Bunty. I know you're retired but you haven't forgotten everything from your psychotherapy practice."

Bunty relented, as Nell had known she would.

"When I was researching forgery," Nell began, "I read that forgers often want to be caught and lately I've been wondering—it's just a silly thought probably—but I've been wondering if Henry Willoughby might be following that pattern. Wondering if that's why he wants to reveal his identify by publishing this memoir."

Bunty looked thoughtful.

Nell pressed on.

"Something Woodford Stone said when we were in The Grog that day."

Nell frowned, trying to remember.

"Something about Henry's transgressions possibly coming to light. He mentioned arrest or incarceration, and then I said—and I remember saying this, and sounding very haughty when I said it—I think he's quite prepared for anything like that. But I don't know why I said that, Bunty, and now I'm wondering if I was prescient. I'm wondering now if it could be true."

"What would you do if that were the case?" Bunty was using a crisp, professional tone.

The question surprised Nell into silence. Bunty waited.

"I'm thinking," Nell said slowly, "that maybe I am a cog in the machine of his capture, could that be? Maybe Henry chose me as part of his plan. I might be the means for revealing his life of crime. After all, I'm the one writing the memoir—the tool of revelation. Is he using me, d'you think?"

She was stumped. Bunty waited.

"I could refuse to continue the memoir," she said, thinking aloud. "Refuse to give it to Robert. Henry would have no recourse. He doesn't have the electronic files—he doesn't even have a computer."

Bunty continued to wait.

"Or," Nell said slowly, "we could just go ahead and publish and let the chips fall where they may."

"Even if it means seeing Henry go to jail?"

Nell shuddered.

"Except he'd call it gaol," she said. "But yes, even that."

"There is one other thing you could do."

"What?"

"Just ask him."

CHAPTER 36

Henry Willoughby's blessing at last! Nell had caught every stitch of change Henry had requested, and he finally pronounced the manuscript finished.

"What's next?" he wanted to know.

"We turn the files over to my friend Robert Hutchins," Nell told him, "and Robert will turn it into a proper book. There will still be things for you to do. A designer will prepare cover art, and you will have choices and decisions to make. Good ones, though. Fun things. You'll be asked consider book design. This should make you feel right at home, Henry. This stage will be great fun."

Henry Willoughby was delighted.

"And," Nell continued, "Robert will use print-on-demand to publish, so you can order as many copies or as few as you wish. He'll put it on Amazon and you can market it. Put ads in all the art publications you follow."

Nell watched a faint cloud pass over Willoughby's face. She waited for him to gather his thoughts and explain.

"Stone..." he began.

Nell looked up.

"What about him?"

"Stone...can't do anything now, can he? It's too late for him to..."

"To what?" Nell asked sharply.

When Henry didn't reply, Nell grew sharper still.

"Henry, has Stone been around again? You didn't tell me."

"He did pay me a short visit, " Henry admitted. "He wanted to know where we were in the publishing process."

You didn't..."

"No, no, no, I didn't let on," Henry hurried to say. "I intimated that we were stalled. Weren't sure what we were going to do. Then I lied about the publication date. Said we'd pushed it off for a while. That mollified him. I think he believed his little intimidations scared us off, at least for a time."

Nell considered this. It was probably a good tactic. She thought it was very clever of Henry.

"Anyhow, he went on his way without much ado, and I think my fib bought us a little time."

But Henry Willoughby suddenly brightened.

"Now that we are nearly finished, my dear, there is something I've been wanting to give you—apart from my final payment, of course, which is just about due. Come."

He led Nell deep into the manse and took from the wall a small oil painting. It was a portrait of a child—an oil sketch, although one Nell had never noticed before, Still, it seemed somehow familiar. She murmured that as she studied it.

"I thought it might," Henry said. "I did this painting from the pencil sketch of Charlotte Amberson as a child—the one I found and used as reference for the Sargent. I wanted you to have a painting of mine—a true painting, not a forgery—and I finally decided that this little portrait might have special meaning. Might remind you of what we shared and our little adventure together."

Nell was too overwhelmed to speak. For a second tears gathered. She blinked them away, but when she raised her eyes to Henry, they were shining. She cast both arms about his shoulders and placed a careful kiss on one rosy cheek.

"Henry, this is a true treasure. And possibly the nicest gift I've ever received. I will prize it beyond imagining."

CHAPTER 37

"Your Mr. Willoughby," Robert had said, "is a criminal."

His words kept turning up in Nell's mind at the most uncomfortable moments. If that's true, she thought, then I am aiding and abetting him and that makes me a criminal too. The thought was horrifying.

Ever since Robert had said it though, she had been trying to kick the thought back into the depths of her mind. Go away! Leave me alone! But here it came back again and what was she to do? The legal answer, of course, was clear. March into the Pingree Cabot Museum and reveal the forgery to the director. Then, whatever the museum chose to do with the information was up to them, and Nell was off the hook. She couldn't be held responsible for their action. Or could she? Could she play the noble innocent and see Henry Willoughby arrested, brought to trial and possibly sentenced to jail time? Where was the moral correctness in that?

The scales of ethics in Nell's mind tipped back and forth. Finally, she went to the bookcase and pulled out her copy of

Situation Ethics. What is the most loving thing to do in any situation? That was the question that one was supposed to ask.

Well then, that settled it. She would stand by Henry and if the PCM had not done proper due diligence and had purchased a fake, then caveat emptor—buyer beware.

But the Pingree Cabot Museum drew Nell as inexorably as the moon draws the tide. The painted figure of Charlotte Amberson seemed to hold secrets that she might be on the verge of revealing if Nell just studied, for enough time, the slight play of a smile around Charlotte's mouth and the something in her eyes that teased merrily. Henry Willoughby had done amazing work. Nell could see that. In great, heavy art books, she had looked up pictures of *Vernon Lee* and *Madame Gautreau Drinking a Toast* and had seen for herself how these women came alive in Sargent's oil sketches. Henry Willoughby's *The Ethereal Charlotte Amberson*, Nell felt, was every bit the equal of *Vernon Lee*. And Nell wasn't just being prejudiced in Henry's favor either. No, in fact, she could be quite critical, even inclined to lean *away* from a presumed favorite. Gazing at the portrait, Nell could understand why the PCM had purchased it.

She wandered the museum, visiting other galleries and exhibits. She lingered in the museum store and even bought a postcard of *The Ethereal Charlotte Amberson*, and one of those enameled magnets with a reproduction in miniature. The woman behind the glass counter smiled approval at Nell's purchase.

"Our John Singer Sargent," she told Nell. "We are so proud to own it."

"It is exceptional," Nell murmured. She indicated the card and magnet in her hand. "I hope these will remind me."

Wandering, Nell kept alert, expecting to see Elizabeth

Beaman by chance, and at the same time, dreading a sight of the young curator. And then, in the atrium, she did see her— wearing a simple black sheath today and in animated conversation with two other people. She did not see Nell.

Nell dallied beside one of the iron tables outside the atrium's coffee shop. Perhaps Elizabeth Beaman would conclude her conversation. Perhaps she would walk in Nell's direction. And if she did, and if circumstance offered the opportunity, would Nell be enticed to speak further about the Charlotte Amberson? She teased herself with the possibility of this encounter.

But Nell was spared that temptation. Elizabeth Beaman did finish her conversation and with a small farewell wave to the couple she'd been speaking with, and without a glance toward the coffee shop, she hurried off to the stairs that would lift her higher into the museum where her office was. She moved swiftly and lightly and took the stairs two at a time.

CHAPTER 38

Anthony Doheny apparently meant business. Just as Henry Willoughby had predicted, he set his minions to scouring the files of the Midwest Museum of Modern Art, examining receipts for every painting the museum had acquired. Every file was turned out and the authentication for each and every purchase was scrutinized. It came to light that the Pollock wasn't the MMMA's only forgery. A Rothko and three lesser paintings also tested positive for fraud. The Pollock however, and one of the lesser works, had been acquired through one Woodford Stone of Boston, Massachusetts, a registered art certifier. Doheny contacted The Association of Certified Fraud Examiners. Then he called the F.B.I. Art Crimes Team.

Henry Willoughby read all about the MMMA affair in the art publications he received. He was avid for details.

"Every curator and museum director in the country, private and public, will soon be deep in the dingles of their files, and any acquisition with Woodford Stone's fingerprints will be brought before the Inquisition," he reported to Nell.

"Every modern art collector who has done business with Stone, will be in a panic, scrambling to see if their investments are valid or worthless."

He seemed mildly entertained. Nell, however was aghast.

"What if that finger pointing at Stone keeps on pointing and goes straight to you, Henry? I mean, you're known to work with Stone, aren't you? Guilt by association at the very least."

"I'm not the only pony in Woodford's stable," Henry told her. "Stone has a covey of artists and he matches our talents to his tasks. I never touched a Pollock. No, my dear, I'm not worried. Besides, the artist is the invisible man. A man in Stone's position doesn't go squealing about his talent. Indeed, no."

But Nell *was* worried. If the experts at the PCM scented smoke on the wind, it could be just a matter of time before they started looking for fire—started looking into their relationship with Woodford Stone, and one day—one day— the doubting eye was bound to land on *The Ethereal Charlotte Amberson*.

Nell alternately alarmed herself with these thoughts, then talked herself off the ledge. While the portrait's connection to Woodford Stone could be easily recognized, the hand behind the brush wasn't known. And the forger couldn't be identified unless...well, there was one thing...unless Woodford Stone vindictively implicated Henry.

Alarmed once more, Nell wished she'd been less combative and more accommodating to Stone that afternoon in The Grog.

In the meantime, she was hatching a scheme to save Henry Willoughby.

CHAPTER 39

Henry Willoughby had a sister. Muriel Willoughby something-or-other. What was it?

Oh, well never mind. He had a younger sister whom he had not seen in years. A sister who lived in the south of France. A sister who was married to a wealthy man. Nell had heard Henry say he would love to see Muriel once more.

Good.

Nell was working on a plan: She would convince Henry to skip the country. Flee to the south of France and into sanctuary with Muriel and what's-his-name. She envisioned Henry's escape happening at night in a very Casablanca setting. The tarmac wet, the plane grumbling in its impatience to taxi, the authorities closing in.

But wait! Authorities! How would Henry get out of the country if he were a wanted man by the time of his escape? His passport would be on some criminals' detainee list, and he could be tripped up by the TSA.

Oh well, that would be easy. As a forger, he could simply

write his own passport and slip past the authorities. Nell's imagination had Henry on the move again.

Fine. Now Nell saw Henry, forged passport in hand, boarding that plane heading for France.

But wait. Henry has balked, refusing to leave the manse and The Shop and all the paints and brushes, pens and inks therein. All his beloved *lares* and *penates*.

Oh well, Nell would promise to guard them. And Henry's house was just a few miles from Nell's. She could handle that until it was safe for Henry to return.

But what if it were never safe? What if he had to live forever as an expat—a fugitive from justice? Live like a pensioner on the good will of Muriel and whatever-his-name-is?

Oh well, thought Nell Bane, those are just details; the first thing is to get Henry to agree to the escape.

Henry Willoughby did not agree. He listened, he laughed, and then he told Nell that she was a dear, dear girl, but this was all completely unnecessary. He would be fine, just fine.

"But you want to see Muriel," Nell argued.

"Someday," Henry said. "Someday."

"Someday will never come," Nell told him with some heat, "if you are in jail."

Henry Willoughby laughed again.

"What will happen, will happen," Henry was sanguine. "No fear."

CHAPTER 40

What would happen would happen, as Henry had said, but Nell was a feasibility tester. Had been one all her life. And she wanted to *know* what would happen so she could be better prepared. And who knew? Maybe she could change the course of things so the worst outcome wouldn't come rattling down upon their heads.

Forgery is an economic crime—she accepted that. Here were private collectors and institutions paying enormous sums for pieces of art that were not what they were represented to be. And she realized that the high prices that were being demanded for art—both real and fake—had fueled the cause of forgery by making it lucrative. There was money to be made. Huge amounts of it. And Nell, a law-abiding citizen, also understood that the law had to be served.

And so, Bunty Whitney found Nell swotting away at her kitchen counter—where Nell did everything from ghostwriting to soup making—and she didn't look happy.

"What are you doing now?"

"Worrying, mainly. Bunty, I've just realized that Henry could go to prison for forgery, and I'm trying to understand what could happen to him."

"Well, duh," was Bunty's response. "You've just figured that out *now*? In what paper bag have you been keeping your head?"

"Listen to this," Nell said, ignoring Bunty's sarcasm and consulting a sheet she'd downloaded. "These two guys in Germany cobbled up something called *The Hitler Diaries*—one guy forged the documents and the other convinced the media that the thing was real. They sold it to *Stern* for something like 9.3 million. Well, euros, I guess."

Bunty issued an impressed whistle.

"What happened to them?"

"Prison!" Nell told her. "They were sentenced to four-and-a-half years each."

"Did they have to give back the dough?"

"I don't know," Nell said, "I would think so, though. This article doesn't say."

Bunty seated herself on the stool next to Nell and leaned in to better see the papers Nell was studying.

"Oh, and here's another one," Nell said. "Wolfgang Beltracchi—this guy has *chutzpah* in spades."

"Another German," she added in an aside to Bunty.

"He claims that he's forged hundreds of paintings in an international art scam and has earned millions of euros. He was brought to trial but only accused of forging fourteen paintings but even that netted roughly forty-five thousand."

"A mere pittance," Bunty murmured.

"His trial lasted forty days," Nell told her, "and Beltracchi served just over three years in prison. Oh, and he had to make restitution, but apparently that was no problem, because when he got out of prison, he was so famous that he went legit and became even wealthier."

"Crime does pay," Bunty declared, pounding the counter with her fist. "I always suspected it did."

"And this poor fellow. Han van Meergren."

"Another German? Wow."

"Dutch," Nell told her.

"In 1945 he was charged with selling Dutch treasures to the Nazis. So he went to trial and his defense was that he'd sold them forgeries. You'd think they'd have let him off with congratulations, but no. The court in Amsterdam found him guilty anyway and sentenced him to prison for a minimum of one year. He died of a heart attack, though before he could serve his time."

"So he got the last word," Bunty added editorially.

"But this is the interesting one," Nell continued, ignoring Bunty. "I was just reading about him when you came in. John Myatt. A Brit. I've run across his name before and it's always connected with his partner. The one who promotes the art and certifies it," she explained to Bunty.

"Well, he interests me because this partner reminds me of Woodford Stone. The fellow's name is John Drewe and it seems he may have led Myatt, who was a struggling but legitimate artist, down the path of crime. Myatt was eventually arrested by Scotland Yard, but he volunteered to return the money he'd earned—in six figures, by the way—in order to help convict Drewe. He'd figured out that Drewe was a rat and a greedy criminal sort of rat.

"So Scotland Yard goes to Drewe's house and finds evidence of all kinds of forgery stuff, you know, to forge certification of authenticity and links to Myatt and so forth. Then Myatt and Drewe both go to trial. Myatt got a year's sentence and served four months, but Drewe got six years for conspiracy."

Nell turned to Bunty with horror in her eyes.

"What if...what if they arrest Henry for...

"For what?"

"Well, for forgery. For conspiracy to defraud! They could send him away. I couldn't bear it!"

"Look at the bright side," Bunty counseled. "These sentences for forgery don't seem too long. What, about a year? And with time off for good behavior? Henry would certainly behave himself, so he'd probably get out early."

"Bunty!" Nell was scandalized. "He's an old man. Time isn't on his side. And that dear little man in prison? Think what they might do to him!"

"What about Stone?" inquired Bunty, continuing to play devil's advocate. "Don't you care what happens to him?"

"Stone!" Nell spat the name. "No I don't care. He deserves the worst. And if the worst happens, he's earned it. I hope whatever happens to him, happens.

Without realizing it, Nell had echoed Henry Willoughby.

CHAPTER 41

The man who forged the MMMA's Jackson Pollock was called Barrett Suggs. His identity was exhumed, and he was arrested in Passaic, New Jersey. And with him, Woodford Stone was also arrested and charged as an accomplice in the forgery of the MMMA's ersatz Jackson Pollock.

This was newsworthy enough to carry into the mainline media, if only briefly, but it made enough noise that Willoughby and even Nell, and even Nell's artier friends such as Ann Fitzmaurice and Bunty Whitney, got the news.

Nell's glimpse of this Suggs, in a blurred, low-res photo, was enough to send her reeling through Google for more information.

"He looks just like he sounds," Nell told Bunty and Ann. "Greasy. Arrogant. Tattoos on every inch of showing skin. He looks like one of his own forged Jackson Pollocks."

Nell had learned a few things about ink from a brief, but annoying acquaintanceship, with a sixteen-year-old named Indigo Eton, the great-granddaughter of clients.

"Surly," Nell continued, as she recalled Suggs's remarks to a reporter following his arrest.

But now that Suggs and Stone had been arrested and arraigned, Nell knew that a forger as well as the certifying accomplice could be held accused and put on a fast track toward trial. And this renewed her concern for Henry.

Nell returned to Google, to Wikipedia and to YouTube. Barrett Suggs's studio, she reported, was above an auto repair shop.

"Very convenient," Bunty remarked caustically. "He didn't have to go far to get his materials. He could share with his downstairs neighbors."

Based on what she'd seen online, Nell could tell that the studio walls were thick with works of his art—enormous, stretched canvases heavy with layers of paint.

"More colors than Joseph's coat," Nell said wonderingly, describing what she had seen, "and he applies the paint with a bricklayer's float. Trowels it on. And he proudly describes what he's doing while he trowels. I saw him on YouTube. I think he actually believes that what he's doing is serious art. It's *dreck*."

"*Dreck*?" Bunty repeated. "Nell, dear, your language has slipped."

But Nell, discussing the Suggs arrest with Henry Willoughby, once again brought up her plot to escape to the south of France. This time Henry seemed to consider it. He looked worried, Nell thought.

Taking pity on the old man, Nell invited him to lunch at the Black Cow in Newburyport.

"And afterwards, I'll take you to Backstreet Guild of Artists and Craftsmen."

Henry was pleased. "I'd like that very much, my dear."

CHAPTER 42

As a last minute inspiration, Nell invited Robert Hutchins to join them, and he was waiting for them at The Black Cow.

"Good to see you again, Henry." Robert rose and shook Henry Willoughby's hand warmly.

"And you as well," Henry replied. "I so much enjoyed meeting you and the rest of Nell's friends at Thanksgiving. For me, it was a real joyful occasion."

"Nell and I have always especially liked this booth," Robert said, indicating the nook by the window that was clad in shiplap siding and overlooked the turbulent Merrimac River. "I understand your manuscript is just about finished and therefore ready for me to take over. Are you excited?"

Henry was.

"I suppose it will be a while for the typed pages to turn into an actual book," he said. "I'll try to be patient."

"You won't have to be patient for very long," Robert told him. "Thanks to technology—specifically print-on-demand—its is simply a matter of prepress work and an upload to the printer."

"Ah." Henry nodded significantly to Nell. "This is one of those cases where technology is one's friend,"

He directed his attention to Robert.

"I explained to Nell at one point that technology has obsoleted a number of my...ah... business segments. Cut into my profit margin and forced me to look to...well...to other pastures in which to graze."

He smiled mysteriously. "But we won't discuss those pastures in law-abiding company."

"I won't press you then," Robert said, "but perhaps we'd like to order?"

It was a happy lunch. And Nell, seeing that her client was so thoroughly enjoying himself, felt warmed and happy as well. Henry Willoughby was such a merry little fellow, and she felt he didn't get out to be around people as much as he'd like. This is good for him, she thought.

Robert Hutchins insisted on picking up the tab for lunch.

"It's no more than a publisher should do," he told Nell and Henry over their protests. Both had planned to stand treat.

"Very kind indeed," Henry told him. "But when will I see you again? Soon, I hope."

"I expect there will be a congratulatory book launch party, if Nell is up to her usual form."

"I believe in celebrations," Nell said firmly. "*The Gallery of Rogues* should be no exception. But now, Henry, we have a date to visit Backstreet Guild of Artists and Craftsmen. Are you joining us, Robert? Ann and Bunty will to be very disappointed if they knew you were in Newburyport and didn't visit."

"Those are two ladies I would not want to disappoint," Robert said suavely. "Lead on."

Bunty and Ann Fitzmaurice greeted Henry as cordially as

Robert had. Nell watched as Bunty took his arm in a proprietary manner and led him about the shop accompanied by Ann who was prepared to discuss each painting. Henry had a number of questions and comments.

The week before, Nell had brought Henry's gift of the oil sketch to Ann, proud to display her treasure.

"I can't take my eyes off this," Ann had said. "Such life. Amazing brushwork."

Nell was gratified.

"I feel very fortunate to have it," she had said humbly.

Now, as Bunty drew Henry off to see her pottery— furnishing him with lavish details of clay and glaze—Ann drifted to Nell's side.

"He was very complimentary about our paintings," Ann whispered. "I was actually nervous."

"Well, he means it!" Nell told her earnestly. "And the shop looks wonderful. Congratulations yet again."

CHAPTER 43

Woodford Stone, Henry had learned—he was following these things avidly and keeping Nell informed—had been arraigned along with Barrett Suggs, was now out on bail and was not deemed a flight risk. Nevertheless, he fled as far as Newburyport, where Nell found him in the middle of an otherwise pleasant afternoon when she answered the doorbell.

"Hells, bells and doorbells!" she had said when the chimes musically announced a visitor. It was her standard response, for Nell didn't much like surprises and her friends generally went around to the back door, expecting her to be in the kitchen.

"Good afternoon, Mrs. Bane." Stone's cold tone and demeanor belied his polite greeting. "I'd like to come in and have a few words with you."

Nell was aware of her beating heart. She didn't usually notice her heart. She stepped outside so she was on the step with him, and she closed the door firmly behind her.

"I'd rather you didn't," she said, keeping her voice as firm as the closed door, "but if you have something to say, you may tell me here."

Woodford Stone scowled, but he continued.

"I have been to see Willoughby," he began. "He tells me that his damnable book is back on track, about to be published, in fact. Is that correct?"

Nell refused to reply and Stone waited. When he saw she didn't intend to say anything, he continued.

"I couldn't get anywhere with the stubborn fellow, so I decided to see if you were more sensible."

Nell's continued silence was like a wall. Woodford Stone appeared to be estimating it.

"I want that book stopped! I don't care where it is in the publishing process—on the presses, being packed into cartons for shipping—I don't care, but I want it halted!"

His voice was very quiet, but to Nell it sounded like the early warning sounds a wild animal makes just before a growl bursts into a savage snarl, Stone's eyebrows grew darker as they rushed to meet over the bridge of his nose. As he had in the encounter in Henry's driveway, Stone pushed his face so close to hers that she could smell—what? A whiff of garlic? Decay? The hint of brimstone underneath his cologne?

"If. This. Book. Is. Published," he spat. "If it comes out, it will implicate me in an affair that will make the Jackson Pollock thing out in Ohio look like a scandal in a nursery school."

He paused and drew his face back from hers.

"Are you listening?" he demanded. "Are you following what I'm saying?"

Nell remained impassive.

"I am going down for the Pollock thing. Okay. I'll take my medicine. But that's all I'll take. A few months in prison. A fine. But no more—that and no more, do you understand?"

Nell crossed her arms across her chest and boldly looked Woodford Stone in the eye.

"I understand," she replied very quietly, "but I can do nothing. The memoir belongs to Henry. He is the only one with the power to stop it."

"I don't know why Willoughby isn't concerned for his hide, but he isn't," Stone said. "Senile maybe. Yes, that's probably it. Too old to care. Thinks he's too old to be sent to prison. But you wouldn't like to see that happen, would you? An old man like that trying to make his way in prison?"

A thought seemed occur to Woodford Stone. Something lightened in his face.

"You could be implicated too, Mrs. Bane. You've been ghostwriting his story for quite some time. That means that for a long while you've known of the Charlotte Amberson forgery. You've been withholding information on a criminal activity, and if there's a trial, you'll be in the thick of it. Probably have legal troubles of your own. You'd better get a good lawyer, Mrs. Bane. You'll swing with us, all three together."

Nell unfolded her crossed arms and let them hang at her sides.

"Sorry to disappoint you, Mr. Stone, but I'm not going to do anything about this. That's final."

Again his frown.

"Do you remember we spoke of consequences, Mrs. Bane? It may be time to put some teeth into that promise. I have thought about this and have realized the only way to influence Henry Willoughby is through you. If something were to happen to *you*, Mrs. Bane, Willoughby might see the light."

"Is that a threat, Mr. Stone? One of the consequences?"

"You could call it either," Stone gave a bark of sardonic laughter. "Or both."

He turned—almost pirouetted—and skipped down the front walk with the same panther-like grace she'd seen last winter in Henry's driveway.

Nell stewed. After Woodford Stone's hunter-green jag disappeared down the street, Nell paced the little house, fretfully, talking to herself. Trying to calm herself.

"I'm suffering post-traumatic syndrome," she said. Still, she was proud of the way she'd behaved when Stone threatened. She hadn't let him know he'd intimidated her. Even though he had.

The interior argument lasted into the next day, and she finally convinced herself to go to the Newburyport police station and discuss the matter. Bill was off duty or out on patrol or whatever, and Nell was disappointed that he wasn't in. She had imagined herself telling him all about the encounter. She and Bill had a history together around this thing, and she felt she could count on his reassuring presence.

The officer at the desk, probably sensing that she was about to bolt, insisted on asking questions though, and those led to other questions and before Nell knew it, she was sitting in a wooden chair, leaning on a desk and initiating a restraining order against one Woodford Stone of Boston.

CHAPTER 44

Henry Willoughby was cheerful. More cheerful than Nell had ever seen him. He mentioned in an offhand way that Stone had paid him a call, but he dismissed this with a wave of his hand and went on to talk about the subject that was his obsession at the moment—his book. It did not occur to him, it seemed, that Nell might have also had a visit from Woodford Stone. Nell decided not to tell him.

As Nell had predicted, Henry was intensely interested in the cover design. Robert Hutchins's graphic designer had generated nearly a dozen concepts and adjustments before Henry was satisfied.

"One thing I'll say for him though," was Robert's ironic comment, "when he does settle on something, he backs it one hundred percent. His enthusiasm is gratifying."

The first proof copy was off the press and Henry received it with the awe and tenderness of a father holding his firstborn.

"Read it carefully," Nell told him. "You will see things in the typeset copy that you didn't see in the computer printouts.

There will be little things to catch and correct, and you may even want to change some words or phrases."

"Isn't it too late?" Henry's forehead puckered with worry.

"Welcome to the world of print-on-demand," Nell told him with a sweeping gesture. "Just indicate the changes and Robert will handle them. And you can keep ordering proof copies until you are completely sure everything is just as you want it."

Henry's proofing process was long. Nell pictured him holed up inside the manse, red pen in hand, reading about his life as a forger and his place among the other forgers in his imaginary gallery.

In the meantime, she had the ominous sensation of being followed. It was unnerving and the haunted feeling interfered with her life. She was reluctant to go out in the evenings, and when she did go out, she looked around her carefully—watching—imagining shapes and seeing shadows where they probably didn't even exist. But sometimes the back of her neck would prickle or the hairs on her forearms would rise. Brimstone? Come on! It's just Woodford Stone, not Old Scratch.

CHAPTER 45

"You're looking very dapper today," Nell told Henry Willoughby.

Henry had invited himself to tea. This had brought Nell up short. She couldn't remember the last time she had entertained a guest for tea. For coffee, yes. That was easy. Just pull out a couple of Bunty Whitney's hand-thrown pottery mugs and a few slices of coffee cake, and you were all set. But tea. Nell thought of bone china cups, the silver sugar basin and pitcher, those tiny spoons tucked away in the silver chest. But she had risen to Henry's self-invitation and dusted off her mother's teapot. She thought about offering digestive biscuits but settled for Pepperidge Farm cookies.

"This seems very formal," she said, handing Henry his cup and saucer.

"It is rather," he replied, "but it is an occasion. I have something very important to say."

Nell smiled and waited.

Henry took a sip of tea, then sat back on the sofa in the snug. This involved setting the cup and saucer down and squirming backwards among the cushions. His legs dangled.

"Now that the *My Place in the Gallery of Rogues* is complete, I am ready to carry out the next step in my plan."

Nell was surprised. She knew nothing of this next step, let alone a plan. An invisible sort of antenna sprang up in the back of her head. She could feel it.

"I am going to tell the people at the Pingree Cabot Museum that *The Ethereal Charlotte Amberson* is a forgery," Henry Willoughby announced. "Tell them that it isn't, as they believe, the work of John Singer Sargent."

Nell was jolted to her core.

Several retorts raced like frightened mice through her mind: You can't do that! Do you know what could happen? Oh but, you can't do that! Finally, she was able to frame a single question:

"Why?"

"Ah," said Henry Willoughby. He smiled angelically.

"I am an old man. Nearing the end of my life, I suppose. There is some settling to do. Last things."

"Last things!" Nell cried, objecting strongly to Henry's tack. "We're not talking eschatology here, surely?"

"No, no, not quite," he said, "but there are some things to clean up. At this point I have my published memoir. And I feel I can rightfully take my place in the gallery of professional forgers who have owned up to their crimes and paid whatever debts they owe."

Nell was still protesting.

"Debts! Do you understand what that could mean? It could mean prison! Terrible fines! They could take your house, Henry!"

The little man shrugged. "If that's the case, so be it. I have no one to come after me. No one to inherit the manse. Muriel certainly doesn't want it. She has everything she needs in

France."

Nell sat for a few minutes in stunned silence. Henry used the silence to squirm forward on the sofa and retrieve his tea cup. He helped himself to a Pepperidge Farm cookie and nibbled delicately on its edge.

Nell took a deep breath.

"What are you going to do?"

"I am going to make an appointment with the director of the PCM," he said. "I am going to his office and I'm going to confess."

"I," said Nell Bane firmly, "am going with you. No," she added, seeing he was about to protest. "This is not negotiable. I *insist* on going with you!"

CHAPTER 46

Nell, trying to match her pace to Henry Willoughby's, was experiencing a petrifying case of stage fright. Her nerves, on edge since Henry disclosed his intention to confess his forgery to the director of the Pingree Cabot Museum, had grown increasingly strung out after Henry secured an appointment with Edward Glendenning. Driving to the PCM, she'd gripped the steering wheel so hard her fingers turned white although the grip did keep her hands from shaking. Once again Nell slowed her pace to Henry's. He had encumbered himself with an enormously awkward artist's portfolio that flapped and threatened to trip either Nell or Henry himself. Nell had knocked into it several times and Henry had dropped the thing twice.

"What's in there?" she had asked, unable to keep the peevish tone out of her voice.

But Henry's reply was mumbled and hadn't made much sense.

Edward Glendenning's office was an aerie at the top of

the museum where interior windows gave views down through the atrium and into the museum's busy main floor. Even in her nervous state, Nell was able to appreciate the magnificence of the space. She imagined herself as a bird soaring into the museum's clear, higher reaches. Upward she soared, shedding her nervousness as she flew into freedom from this office and from the scene that was about to take place here.

Elizabeth Beaman was in the office also, and it was she who welcomed them. She was wearing slacks today, beautifully tailored slacks, Nell noticed, and shoes with heels of amazing height. They showed Elizabeth's slender ankles to good advantage, but Nell couldn't imagine walking in them. Elizabeth Beaman seemed to manage very well though. She didn't even totter on the thick carpet as she escorted them across the office.

Edward Glendenning rose with a welcoming smile as he came around the desk.

"A pleasure to meet you, Mr. Willoughby," he said, offering his hand, "Welcome. I must say, you sounded very mysterious in your phone call."

"It was not a matter for the telephone," Henry replied formally. "I'll get right to the point now, although first I'd like you to meet my friend Mrs. Bane."

"Nell. Please," she said shaking Glendenning's hand. She turned to Elizabeth Beaman. "We've met however. That day in the museum?"

"Yes, indeed," said the young woman, "I remember you very well."

Glendenning seated everyone in a conversation area—a miniature living room—at one end of his office. He and Elizabeth Beaman looked at Henry expectantly.

Nell experienced a new jolt of nerves. She couldn't imagine how Henry would begin.

He got right to it.

"It is my unpleasant task to inform you that one of the paintings in your museum is a forgery."

This was greeted with shocked silence.

Eventually, Glendenning spoke in a quiet voice.

"Please continue."

Henry did. He explained who he was and that it was he who had painted the oil sketch of Charlotte Amberson—the sketch that Stone had represented as a John Singer Sargent and that the museum had purchased.

This admission was met with continued silence—a stunned sort of silence—from Glendenning and Elizabeth Beaman.

They don't believe him, Nell realized suddenly.

Henry didn't seem to care whether they believed him or not. He continued to sit on Glendenning's white sofa, his toes not quite touching the gray carpet. His expression was blissful. In the silence that stretched on, Nell's thoughts caromed about her head, ricocheting off the walls of her skull, scattering information. They think he's touched, she thought—a harmless, possibly senile old man. Her impulse was to defend Henry, and she thought of leaping into the silence to do so, but she could think of nothing to say. She shot him what she hoped was an imperative look. Go on! She willed her thought into his head.

And suddenly Henry hauled up the portfolio.

"I brought some of the working materials for the portrait," he said. "In here."

He indicated the portfolio which promptly slid off his knees. Elizabeth Beaman retrieved it and kindly restored it to Henry's lap. With her help, he got the portfolio open finally and Elizabeth helped him spread the materials on the coffee table. Edward Glendenning leaned forward to examine these.

Elizabeth's pretty chestnut hair obscured her face as she joined him.

Nell and Henry waited.

"This is...?" Glendenning's question drifted off.

"An original pencil sketch of Charlotte as a young child," Henry supplied. "The formal portrait her father had hoped for, was never painted, but there did exist this crude drawing. I dug it out of a musty archive and it was helpful in establishing a few things about Charlotte. The general shape of her face, her eye, so forth."

"And these?" with a gesture, Glendenning indicated a sheaf of drawings.

"Intermediate sketches. Studies. Trial and error things. I thought they might be helpful in establishing that the painting is a true forgery." Henry chuckled. "I hoped to provide provenance for a forgery."

He seemed quite amused at the concept.

Glendenning and Elizabeth Beaman continued to sort through the work.

Henry cleared his throat.

"Perhaps if we visited the portrait, in the gallery," he said timidly, "I could establish absolute proof."

Edward Glendenning immediately rose. Nell and Elizabeth did also.

"Lead on," he said to Henry, "Lead on, Mr. Willoughby, by all means."

"Have you heard of time bombs?" Henry asked when the four of them stood shoulder to shoulder in front of *The Ethereal Charlotte Amberson*.

Glendenning nodded, but Elizabeth Beaman frowned.

"It is a deliberate hint," Willoughby explained to her kindly, "a clue that is meant to prove a particular painting is a fake. It's usually an anachronism, something like the use of a paint that had not been invented at the time the work was supposed to have been created. Forgers do this on purpose sometimes simply because it amuses them, although I suppose the clumsier ones—the clueless ones—do it from ignorance."

The foursome regarded the painting.

"Here," said Henry. "Look just here."

His forefinger touched a spot in the lower lefthand corner. "I worked in a little Quinacridone Gold there. Just there. Lovely vibrancy and permanence. Do you see it?"

"Ah," Elizabeth Beaman was the one to speak; her tone was hushed, awed. "The quinacridones are a synthetically created pigment. They weren't introduced to artists' paints until 1955. They would have been unavailable when Sargent was painting."

Henry Willoughby smiled.

"Very good, my dear."

He beamed at Elizabeth as a venerable art instructor might smile at a bright student.

Nell was scrutinizing the painting.

"I don't see anything," she complained. "I don't know what you're talking about."

"No," Henry told her. "Your naked eye wouldn't be able to see it. It is just a tiny amount of paint cleverly brushed in. But it's there. A spectrophotometer would be able to detect it, and its presence would inform an expert that this is a forgery."

He turned to Edward Glendenning.

"I don't imagine you were the one to accept this painting?"

"It was acquired on my predecessor's watch," Glendenning admitted. "Phillip was known for being punctilious, but perhaps his appetite for a Sargent caused him to be momentarily careless. He was awfully keen to secure a Sargent before he retired from the PCM. This is rather embarrassing," he concluded.

They turned once again to face the painting, each, perhaps considering.

"Let's wrap up this meeting in my office," Glendenning finally suggested briskly.

And wordlessly, the committee filed into the elevator and rode upward in silence, each staring at the closed doors of the elevator car and each wrapped in private thoughts.

Inside the aerie once more, Nell felt keen to get to the point of action; she wanted to hear what course Edward Glendenning and Elizabeth Beaman intended to take. She practically had to bite her tongue to keep from pushing them into their conclusion.

Edward Glendenning resumed his seat in the conference area, steepled his fingers in a manner than reminded Nell of Robert Hutchins, and appeared to look past his fingers into a nothingness beyond. Then, with a glance at Elizabeth, he spoke.

"I think we need to give some concentrated attention to this matter before we take the next steps."

He shot a sharp look at Henry Willoughby.

"There are legal implications, of course. There is also the matter of verifying the painting's legitimacy—or illegitimacy, as may be the case. You've told us it is a forgery and have provided some good rationale why it might be, but we will want to conduct our own tests, of course."

He paused in thought.

"There is also the matter of how the painting was acquired, which was, I believe through a Mr. Woodford Stone. His name is known to us," Glendenning glanced at Elizabeth for confirmation, "through some reports out of the Midwest Museum of Modern Art out in Ohio."

Nell held her breath.

"For now, Mr. Willoughby, while we take this matter under

advisement, we'll do nothing that need affect you. I suggest you go along as you normally do and wait for us to finish our due diligence and get back in touch with you."

He indicated Henry's materials, still spread over the coffee table.

"I hope we may keep these for our investigation."

He stood.

"And we will be back in touch, I assure you of that."

Edward Glendenning extended his hand.

"I can't believe I am saying this, but thank you, Mr. Willoughby—Henry—for coming forward. While it is very bad news—shocking news—that our valuable Sargent is a forgery, the information about it is also valuable and I applaud you for your honesty—in fact, your bravery—in coming forward."

He turned to Nell.

"It has been very nice to meet you Ms. Bane. I hope to see you again when we next get in touch with Henry. He is fortunate to have a good friend like you. Elizabeth, will you be kind enough to see our guests down to the front desk?

But Henry Willoughby wasn't through.

"Oh!" he cried, "there is one more thing."

He grabbed his portfolio, rummaged inside, and brought out two copies of *My Place in the Gallery of Rogues*.

"My memoir!" he explained, as though introducing the book to two new friends. "I must sign a copy for each of you."

Edward Glendenning and Elizabeth Beaman watched in nonplussed silence while Henry sat back down on the white sofa, uncapped a fountain pen and elaborately calligraphed an inscription to each of them, then, with flourishes, signed his name—Henry Herbert Willoughby.

CHAPTER 47

"It was all very civil," Nell told Bunty Whitney and Ann Fitzmaurice. "I don't mind telling you I was scared practically witless. I was sure they would call the police right there and have Henry arrested, but apparently he—we?—have a grace period."

"A time to fret," Bunty offered unhelpfully. "A time to twist in the wind."

And Nell had to agree. "Yes. A time to contemplate the hammer and wait for its fall."

Nell tried to put the waiting time to good use. She washed windows and walked on the Plum Island beach. She paged through her collection of soup recipes. She took herself to the library and came home with a stack of books she'd always intended to read and had, up to that point, successfully avoided. She was trying to read one of these at eleven-thirty one night when the telephone rang.

Nell jumped. The book dropped with a thud.

She had no idea who could be calling at this uncivilized

hour, but a call this late meant serious business or a wrong number.

There was trepidation in her voice, as she answered.

"Ms. Bane? This is Bill Fahey down at the police station."

Nell's heart pounded harder, but her voice, unaccountably, was steady.

"Good evening."

"We found Woodford Stone outside your house tonight, Ms. Bane, in violation of your restraining order. We've arrested him and have him down at the station. Could you possibly come down and identify him?"

"Now?" Nell asked faintly.

"If you like," Bill continued, "we could send a car for you."

"Oh no," she said, "you shouldn't have to do that. I'll come, of course. Just give me a few minutes to dress and I'll be right along."

"We've been keeping an eye on your house, Ms. Bane," Bill explained when Nell arrived. "There was a green Jag parked out front tonight and it matched your description of Stone's car. There was no one in it, however, and I found Stone just by your back gate. You didn't hear anything? Any sounds?"

"I didn't," Nell admitted. "I was deep in my book, I guess."

"Well, we collared 'im," Bill said grimly. "In clear violation of the order. And once we pulled him in, we discovered there's already an outstanding arrest warrant on 'im."

Nell nodded. "He's out on bail, I guess, accused of a crime against a museum in Ohio. What's going to happen to him?"

Bill Fahey shrugged.

"This is one more black mark against him, is all. It won't do him any favors though. We'll let him go tonight with a stiff warning about that restraining order. I wouldn't think he'd violate it again, but you never know. We'll keep an eye out."

Bill looked gravely at Nell.

"You know," he said, "stalking is about power and control. It's also about revenge. And it is very serious."

He was silent for a moment, letting Nell absorb what he'd said. Then he considered.

"You want to see him? Make sure we've got the right guy?"

But Nell didn't want to see Woodford Stone. And more to the point, she didn't want Woodford Stone to see her. He would be brought to trial soon enough. She hoped he'd be sent away. Far away.

CHAPTER 48

How long could it possibly take? Nell was sure her nerve ends would be frayed to fringe if Edward Glendenning and Elizabeth Beaman didn't come forward soon with a decision about Henry Willoughby's fate. She had read every boring book on her "should read" list, and while she felt some whiff of nobility for her effort, it wasn't sufficient compensation for the feeling in the pit of her stomach. She was growing used to the feeling though, and that couldn't be good, she thought.

Finally, Nell turned to her time-honored cure for all things troubling. She made soup. She decided on vegetable stock—a big pot of it—to store in the freezer. She would then have a supply on hand and stock-making was sufficiently time-consuming to divert her attention from slow time and the hollow feeling in her center.

Nell assembled the ingredients. This was easy. Merely a case of mining the vegetable drawer in the refrigerator and pulling out of the freezer the mix of vegetables and parings saved against the inevitable stock-making day.

Carrots, celery, onions, leeks, parsley, and thyme appeared on the kitchen counter. Nell made a trip to the market for fennel and fresh mushrooms.

She roughly chopped the carrots, celery, onions, leeks, mushrooms and fennel, tossed them lightly with olive oil and spread them on a foil-covered baking sheet. She roasted them in a 425 degree oven until the vegetables were nicely browned.

Nell scraped the browned vegetables into a stockpot and covered them with water. She added herbs—fresh parsley, thyme, and bay leaves. She considered adding kombu or seaweed for added flavor, then tossed in a few whole peppercorns. She decided against adding salt; she'd wait until the stock was finished, then taste.

When the water reached a boil, she skimmed the surface and reduced the stock to a simmer. After it had simmered for several hours, Nell allowed the stock to cool, then she strained it and stored it in freezer containers.

When she was finished, and eight pints of stock were stacked in the freezer, Nell found herself in the same state as when she started. Anxious. And tired of waiting.

CHAPTER 49

Henry Willoughby had news. He announced this to Nell in a phone call and for a moment her heart leaped to fill the hollow place in her midsection. But it was just news about Woodford Stone, and Nell felt hope replaced with the taste of disappointment.

Stone's trial had taken place. Anthony Doheny had come all the way from Perrysburg, Ohio to testify, and the judge had found against Woodford Stone and Barrett Suggs. They had each been found guilty of felony—a more serious crime than a simple misdemeanor—and this earned them each a longer sentence and a season in a state prison.

"Stone will be back in court again," prophesied Henry Willoughby, "if the PCM decides to prosecute."

"Henry," said Nell plangently, "when do you expect to hear from Mr. Glendenning?"

"The day will come, my dear," he replied. "It will come in its own time and it will come soon enough."

And eventually the day did come.

Henry made a date to see Edward Glendenning, and he phoned Nell to give her the details. After suffering spasms of nerves that hit her in splashes like waves hitting a sea wall, Nell decided she was looking forward to the meeting. She wanted to put this behind her. Wanted to know the very worst and to meet it head on.

Nell dressed for the appointment with the greatest care. She wanted to look just right. Smart but subdued. She consulted Ann Fitzmaurice whose taste was impeccable, but she did not ask the advice of Bunty Whitney; dear as Bunty was, she would have had Nell tricked out in an outfit from one of Newburyport's lesser charity shops, and Nell wanted to feel equal to Glendenning's aerie and its tasteful white decorating.

Feeling that she looked her best—or as well as could possibly be expected—Nell found herself back in Edward Glendenning's office. The day was sunny and beyond the glass ceiling was an amazing blue infinity.

Elizabeth Beaman was in blue today too. She had chosen a simple blue linen shift in a delectable shade of periwinkle. One slender wrist wore a gold chain, no thicker than a strand of spider's web. Her chestnut hair waved softly about her shoulders.

Henry and Nell were invited to sit on one of Glendenning's white sofas. Nell put her knees to one side, crossed her ankles and waited. Henry simply let his feet dangle. There were pleasantries. The fine weather was discussed, complimented and the next day's weather was speculated upon. Nell was told that she was looking well. The state of Henry's health was inquired after and established to be sound.

Nell shifted on the sofa, positioned her knees in the opposite direction and recrossed her ankles.

Edward Glendenning coughed editorially.

"Well, I suppose we should get down to business," he said.

"We have had *The Ethereal Charlotte Amberson* examined by an expert from IFAR—International Foundation for Art Research, and by Mr. Charles Correale of ACFE, the Association of Certified Fraud Examiners."

He looked at Nell, and explained as an aside, "These outfits specialize in art detective work. Provenance research. In short, forensics. They employ technologies like x-ray and infrared and other means, but they also are expert at tracing ownership history."

Glendenning turned back to Henry.

"Just as you said, Mr. Correale detected traces of Quninacridone Gold. It is unusual to know in advance what you are looking for, but your revelation about that time bomb made Mr. Correale's work more efficient, which, by the way, translated to better use of the Museum's money. He was able to very quickly and conclusively establish the forgery."

Glendenning paused.

"Mr. Correale was especially interested in Mr. Stone. He already knew of the fellow. As you're aware, the MMMA held back no secrets when they discovered the forged Pollock in their collection. They were generous about alerting every university, museum and private collector to the fraud. We were aware that we'd had dealings with Stone, but we just hadn't gotten down to examining our records. And shame on us for delaying. Anyhow, two other museums, acting on the MMMA's tip, uncovered forgeries in their collections too."

Glendenning turned to Elizabeth Beaman.

"Do you wish to add anything, Liz?"

"We immediately pulled our files on Woodford Stone," she said. "The documentation for the Charlotte Amberson oil sketch goes back quite a few years, but it's all there and there is enough to clearly implicate Stone. Fortunately, Charlotte Amberson is the only dealing the PCM has ever had with

Woodford Stone."

Edward Glendenning smiled.

"Oh, there's one more thing, Henry. Mr. Correale gave you a compliment. He said the oil sketch of Charlotte Amberson was absolutely worthy of John Singer Sargent's name. He said if Sargent hadn't painted it, he should have. Sargent, he stated, would have been proud to be the creator of *The Ethereal Charlotte Amberson.*"

Edward Glendenning and Elizabeth Beaman seemed to have finished all they had to say, but to Nell, they hadn't touched on the most important matter. She took a deep breath.

"What are you going to do?" she asked. "Are you intending to prosecute?"

"We certainly intend to prosecute Woodford Stone," Glendenning replied. "Unfortunately, we'll have to get in line behind the MMMA—well, that case has been adjudicated, I understand—but there are two other institutions that have already filed grievances ahead of us."

Nell waited.

"What about Henry? Are you going to prosecute *him?*"

"We had considered it," Glendenning said slowly, "but then we decided to make lemonade from our lemon."

Seeing Nell's quizzical look, Elizabeth Beaman smiled. She was radiant.

"We plan to feature the painting in a special exhibit," she said, "a forgery exhibit. It's a fascinating topic, forgery, and we feel by spotlighting it, we can put together an exciting exhibition that is completely unique—a fresh, unexpected program that will grab attention. We have several forgeries in storage and we'll bring them out into the light of day."

She smiled, and warming to her subject, continued.

"Forgery is an art in itself. We'll focus on its prevalence throughout centuries, and how it has actually contributed to the advancement of art. We'll do a feature on its influence on economics as well—forgery also has considerable relevance there."

"You know," she confided, "forgery is much more common that most would suppose. Virtually every museum has a number of forgeries in their storerooms, and most also have them hanging, unidentified, in galleries."

"But the centerpiece of the exhibit—the real drawing card—will be our Sargent forgery. That's how we'll promote it. *Our* forgery."

She turned to Henry.

"We are counting on the artist to be present and to be featured right along with his work. We hope you'll consent, Mr. Willoughby."

Nell decided she had never seen a more beautiful young woman. She was awe-struck. She looked at Henry. He was beaming.

"I would be delighted," he said.

CHAPTER 50

Staging a major exhibition in a first rate art museum, as Nell eventually discovered, was an event on a scale with the invasion of Normandy or the inauguration of a twenty-first century president. Elizabeth Beaman, as assigned curator, had been whirling through her days like a well-groomed dust devil. Nell couldn't begin to imagine how she kept all the details straight, but every time Nell popped in to the PCM, Elizabeth looked like she was thriving.

"She looks better every time I see her," she told Bunty. "All the confusion, all the responsibility, all the tiny, maddening details just seem to fuel her energy. She glows."

Nell shook her head.

"And she has envisioned the whole thing—all the exhibits—they already exist in her head. And she has contacted people all over the country."

"Why?" Bunty wanted to know.

"She's borrowing art fakes from everywhere. And what's more, she's convincing other curators and collectors to share their forgeries and tell their stories. And they are doing it, these curators! And loving it apparently. It's sort of like these people are playing a joke on the art community, themselves included. Quite a few of them, in fact, are coming to the opening and looking forward to swapping stories with other curators who have been horn-swoggled. By all accounts, this exhibition is going to be one whale of a party."

"Goody," said Bunty greedily. "Am I going to be invited? To the opening gala, I mean? Not just to walk around the exhibit with the trodden masses later, after all the champagne's been drunk?"

But Nell had that covered. She was looking forward to having not only Bunty Whitney and the Fitzmaurices on the invitation list, but Robert Hutchins and Jerry Gasso too.

"Henry will be over the moon to see all of you," she said. "He's been hinting that another dinner party on a par with Thanksgiving would be lovely."

Nell paused, thinking.

"But I don't know when this gala is going to come off. There is so much to do. I'd had no concept of it all."

But like all things, including childbirth and ripening apples, in the fullness of time, even the Pingree Cabot Museum's major exhibition—*The Art of the Forger*—ripened and was ready to bear fruit.

Advertisements began appearing everywhere, even on public television stations and in pop-up ads on Google. A major Boston news station featured the exhibit and the museum in a four-minute clip on their lifestyle segment. H.H. Willoughby was interviewed for a podcast. Nell was amazed.

Checking frequently with Henry Willoughby, she found anticipation was winding him up like him one of the clocks on the manse's mantel. Henry, for all his solitary life bent over a drawing board, was a convivial soul. He loved parties and he loved people. Nell wondered if anyone had ever given him a birthday party and, fearing a negative answer, was afraid to ask.

She did ask him what he intended to wear to the opening. The polka-dot bowtie he had worn on their first meeting was still bright in her mind.

He looked sheepish and peered up at her from under his eyebrows.

"I would like to wear evening clothes," he admitted shyly.

"Well, that would be very appropriate," Nell told him heartily. "Do you have evening clothes?"

"Not yet," Henry Willoughby said. "But by next week, I will."

"You will look perfect."

And on the gala evening when the Pingree Cabot Museum opened its doors to the exhibition, he did look perfect.

At the north end of H.H. Willoughby, his bald head gleamed and at the south end, his highly-polished black slippers shone. In between, a pair of blue eyes twinkled, a mischievous smile darted, and playing against the type of the severe black tuxedo, was a scarlet bowtie

"Well, at least the tie didn't light up or start playing *Moonlight Sonata*," Jerry Gasso observed.

The team of Nell's friends—now Henry's friends as well—stood in a cluster just inside the atrium, gazing up and around at the amazing work of Elizabeth Beaman.

Banners twelve feet or possibly longer were suspended on invisible wires from the upper regions of the atrium and these drifted down to promote the exhibit and entice the visitors.

The Art of the Forger proclaimed some of the banners. Others featured examples of the art that would be seen inside the exhibit—prime among them was *The Ethereal Charlotte*

Amberson. There was even a banner with a full length picture of Henry Willoughby in a jaunty stance with his arms folded across his chest.

The flesh-and-blood Henry Willoughby crossed the atrium to meet his friends. There were cries of greeting, kisses from Bunty, Ann and Nell, vigorous handshakes and expressions of congratulation from Jerry Gasso, Franklin Fitzmaurice and Robert Hutchins.

Henry, Nell decided, looked happy enough to levitate. She wouldn't have been surprised to see him float right up into the atrium's highest reaches, his little black-shod feet dangling.

"But you must meet Elizabeth!" he cried. "My fairy godmother. Oh, no! Wait! That's you, Nell, you're my fairy godmother."

He paused, looking confused. "Maybe a fellow can have two fairy godmothers? Oh well, never mind. Elizabeth! There are some people I want you to meet."

Moved more than she could express, Nell wandered deeper into the atrium where a party was in full rumble. Tables swathed in long white clothes held silver trays of appetizers and other trays offered glistening fruit-topped tarts and rows of delicate pastel petite fours. Waiters and waitresses in black and white swerved deftly among the guests, balancing trays and glasses and urging guests to try the stuffed mushrooms, the steak with horseradish on warm potato chips, the chicken teriyaki on sticks.

Nell's eyes drifted toward the gallery where the Americana collection was housed, but tonight Charlotte Amberson had left that gallery for another. *The Art of the Forger* was being presented in the museum's mezzanine gallery—a series of connecting rooms that actually bridged a narrow inlet of the atrium. Visitors crossing this bridge were able to look down into the atrium through a floor made of glass.

There was some difficulty moving to the mezzanine stairs though. Henry was stopped and detained every ten feet and his party had to wait while his hand was shaken, congratulations were delivered, his shoulder was punched, and questions were answered. At last, however, they climbed the single flight of stairs, and Jerry Gasso pulled open the door to the first room in the exhibit. Nell, walking through it, was absorbed into another world.

Immediately, voices hushed. They were in a chamber— an enclosure like a jeweler's box with walls of black velvet— and directly before them, and lit from above, was an abstract painting. Streaks of descending reds and blues, yellows and creams, drips like melting paint, vibrated like jeweled necklaces on the huge canvas.

Headlight #7.

Nell caught her breath. The MMMA's Jackson Pollock. Rather, the *forged* Pollock. The work of Barrett Suggs and teamed with the con artistry of Woodford Stone. Nell was no connoisseur of representational art, but still...there was something about this piece that caught her, made her pause, and would make her remember.

She moved to the copy panel next the painting and carefully read. Perhaps it was the presentation. Perhaps the lighting. Perhaps it was just because she knew the history—the provenance—of this piece, but seeing it, overwhelmed her.

She took three steps backward and stood next to Henry Willoughby.

"I didn't expect..." she said.

He slipped his hand under her elbow.

"Some of it is theater, my dear," he said. "Presentation has a lot to do with it. But the painting does have some of the power good art is required to have. And one would expect it to have. After all, the MMMA bought it in good faith and they are not generally fools."

"I never knew automobile paint could be so affecting," she said.

Nell allowed her attention to leave the painting and look at the walls, arranged in four panels to half-embrace the work.

"A Farrow & Ball color?" she whispered.

Henry nodded.

"Black Blue, I'd surmise. Very dramatic. Perfect. That young woman—Elizabeth Beaman—she knows her stuff."

Nell drifted around the end of the semi-wall and into the wider gallery. And here she caught her breath again.

For here, on another half wall, this one painted Chinese Blue, and right in the center of the gallery, was the familiar and lovely *The Ethereal Charlotte Amberson.* As ever, the enchanting character of the young subject, so vital with that hint of mischief, shone with such veracity that Nell had to pinch herself to remember this was just paint.

Charlotte Amberson's story—and Henry Willoughby's as well—was told in detail on the copy board. But visitors were also invited to press a button like a doorbell and hear the voice of H.H. Willoughby telling the story of painting.

A few people were listening intently to the narration while other groups of viewers were admiring the painting from several paces back.

"So this is the famous Charlotte," Bunty Whitney murmured. "Amazing."

Ann Fitzmaurice's appreciation was more technical. She allowed herself to get as close to the painting as possible in order to examine the brushwork. She shook her head. A portraitist herself, her appreciation was professional.

Henry Willoughby was watching her. A small smile, playing about his lips. As Ann stepped back, she caught him watching, and she shook her head. Then, in a very unlike-Ann gesture, she slipped her arm through his and lightly brushed her lips across his cheek.

"Kudos," she said simply. "Marvelous. I am envious."

Henry ducked his head in shy thanks.

They stepped into an area that could have been a typical gallery in a museum anywhere. Oil paintings from the seventeenth and eighteenth century were hung in proper order on walls painted deep terra cotta.

"Book Room Red," Henry murmured to Nell.

"Farrow & Ball?"

"Precisely."

"A Reubens!" Ann gasped, recognizing a small painting in an ornate gilt frame. "That can't be a fake, surely!"

Elizabeth Beaman, who had joined them, raised an eyebrow. "Well, in truth, we can't be too sure."

She smiled at Ann's stunned expression.

"The old masters often had their employees and apprentices work on sections of their work. No one really knows how much of the paintings was the work of these people and how much—indeed, if any—was the work of the master. It was a much more casual world then, and the assistants were excellent artists in their own rights. It is quite possible that a work we attribute to Reubens or Rembrandt was really done by someone else completely. In that sense—in the sense we regard it today—those works are forgeries."

She smiled again, this time enigmatically, and turned away to let Ann Fitzmaurice contemplate this.

From the wall at the end of this gallery—surprisingly among the old masters from past centuries—a vast silkscreened head stared at them.

Elizabeth indicated this.

"It's been suggested that Andy Warhol at his Factory, continued to work like the Renaissance masters. His people created some—and sometimes all—of Warhol's art. But few know who did what and Warhol himself would have been the last to let out the secret. Perhaps you could argue that many Warhols are forgeries, but to the man himself, they were art. And his many collectors, willing to pay what amounts to millions, would apparently agree."

Nell realized that Elizabeth Beaman was highly entertained by the subject of forgery. Part artistic joke, part mystery, she was having a wonderful time gently twitting connoisseurs of all stripes in the art community who generally took themselves very seriously.

Elizabeth's point of view seemed to be shared by a number of honored guests—curators and dealers and collectors. Nell had been peeking at their nametags and they were responding the exhibition with what amounted to delight. Well, that was reasonable, she supposed. If you couldn't appreciate the lighter side of this duplicity, you'd probably have stayed home.

In the hands-on forensic exhibit, which had been furnished with tools for forgery detection, Franklin Fitzmaurice was playing with a black light, passing it back and forth over an overpaint of an eighteenth century landscape.

"Look here," he instructed Jerry Gasso, "See this bright white area? Titanium white. That's the tip-off of a fake."

Jerry, peering over Franklin's shoulder nodded, but forensic technology didn't particularly interest him and he turned to leave.

"Oooh," he heard Bunty Whitney exclaim as she stepped into his spot, "Toys. How does this thing work, Franklin?"

Jerry left Franklin and Bunty murmuring over forensic forgery and moved to the next gallery—the Hall of Forgers. These scoundrels, now, that was right up Jerry's alley.

In the center of this gallery, Jerry found Nell. She was turning slowly, regarding the faces of Henry Willoughby's companions in the brotherhood.

"Han van Meergeren—so aristocratic" she murmured as though she were introducing him. "Wolfgang Beltracchi—looks like a lead guitarist in a rock band—and wealthy as a rock star too, once he got out of jail."

She moved slowly sideways, scanning the portraits.

"Elmyr de Hory," she remarked, turning to Jerry. "He's a hot one. De Hory is credited with almost 1,000 forgeries—forgeries that are so good, that since his death, collectors have been queuing up to pay thousands for them. So good, in fact, that *forged* de Horys have started showing up."

Nell shook her head wonderingly and strolled on, reviewing the rogue's gallery.

"John D. Re," she read. "And oh gosh! Mark Landis. He looks like he could use a shot of Vitamin B12 and a day in the sunshine."

Then, there—in his rightful place in the Gallery of Rogues—there was Nell's very own H.H. Willoughby. Elizabeth Beaman had created a wonderful portrait. Henry's cherubic face emerged from a charcoal background and he twinkled up at the camera, looking more like a fellow who bred angora kittens than a man who'd operated outside the law. Nell felt a warm sense of pride.

But the adjoining gallery featured Forgery's Partners. There were portraits here as well, and biographies dedicated to the upscale pitchmen—the art world's snake oil salesmen—who had scammed the art community with fast talking salesmanship and falsified documents certifying provenance. Without the skill of these con men, forgeries might never take place, These front men have grown wealthy off the talent of the men at the easels.

Nell stopped in front of a photo of John Drewe, the man who 'made' John Myatt. She recalled reading that Myatt had once called his paintings 'appallingly bad' but for Drewe's documentation that made them credible enough to convince art buyers that were masterpieces.

She shook her head, but as she was turning away, she was unexpectedly confronted with a familiar face—the face of Woodford Stone. The feelings that Stone had always generated were instantly ignited, even by his photograph—the banging heart, the sensation of gravity dropping inside her, even that imagined whiff of brimstone.

The background in this photo was black and dappled with spotlights, and out of this ominous half-light, Stone's inscrutable face emerged as he looked looking piercingly into the camera lens. For several uncomfortable seconds, Nell took in his handsome, slightly vulpine face. And his eyes. Always his eyes...

She shivered and glanced at her watch.

"The program down in the atrium will be starting any minute," she told Jerry. "We don't want to be late."

"Certainly not," Jerry agreed. "I wouldn't want some other art lover to grab the last pastry on the platter."

CHAPTER 51

Edward Glendenning and Anthony Doheny had become great friends. Not only had Doheny contributed his ersatz Pollock to the exhibition, but he had insisted upon attending the gala as well, and had made the trip east from Perrysburg Ohio. They made a curious couple, Nell thought. Edward so tall, quiet and scholarly and plump Anthony, short and ebullient, bouncing along at Glendenning's side like an excited puppy. The pair had collaborated on a program, and now a series of chimes sounded around the museum alerting people to the program's start.

"All of us who are active in the art world," Edward Glendenning began, "are aware of the threat—the specter— of forgery. We dread it. We fear it. And yet, we live with it constantly. A late director of the Met once estimated that forty percent of the objects he examined for the museum were fakes. Forty percent! And a senior investigator for the FBI Crimes Team has observed that there are forgeries in every museum— rooms full of them—usually basement rooms but he admitted that sometimes they get into the galleries too.

"Forgeries are embarrassments, proof that we art professionals don't always know what we're talking about. And I'm not just meaning museum directors and curators here."

He threw a meaningful look at his new pal Anthony Doheny who responded with a knowing grin worthy of the Cheshire cat.

"Everyone who has anything to do with art today," Glendenning continued, "—from galleries as grand as the Metropolitan Museum of Art and auction houses as august as Sotheby's down to corner shops where paintings are sold—can be taken in by fakes.

"Well, tonight we took the wraps off forgeries. We threw open our closet doors and owned up to one of the facts of art life. And in so doing, we poked some fun at ourselves. 'See, we said, we're not so smart after all! Like everyone else, we're just human'.

"*However*...and this is an important however ... some fakes or forgeries are good enough to stand on their own merit as art. Some, in fact, are excellent. And you've also seen some of these tonight."

Here Anthony Doheny raised his hand and stepped forward.

"And some," he grinned, "are *not* excellent. And you've seen some these tonight as well. For example, *Headlight #7*, looks good to the naked eye but it won't stand the test of time. In fact, it won't last as long as last year's model Buick."

By now, everyone had learned the provenance of the MMMA's fake Pollack and appreciative laughter ran around the atrium.

Smiling, Doheny stepped back and nodded at Glendenning to continue.

"I want to thank Anthony Doheny for being here tonight,"

Edward said, "because he is actually the whistle-blower who started this whole thing—started it with his disclosure that his Midwest Museum of Modern Art owned a Jackson Pollock forged by Barrett Suggs, a part-time auto parts dealer in Passaic, New Jersey. And the MMMA isn't the only owner of a Pollock fake. They abound in the hundreds.

"Among the forgeries we are unveiling tonight, we are also—and with some pride—introducing a forger. But a very special one. H.H. Willoughby painted an oil sketch called *The Ethereal Charlotte Amberson* which this museum acquired a number of years ago under the impression it was the work of John Singer Sargent. We have been immensely proud to own it. But it came to light recently—well it came to light when Mr. Willoughby himself came in and told us—that the painting was not the work of Sargent. We had his assertion verified by experts from the IFAR and the ACFE, one of whom said that John Singer Sargent would have been proud to have painted *The Ethereal Charlotte Amberson*."

"So while we can all agree that forgery is an economic crime, we can also recognize that it can be true art. We hope our exhibition tonight has brought that fact home.

"Now there is one more thing to say:

"H.H. Willoughby has recently completed a memoir—and I would note he did this with the help of a ghostwriter. Although Mrs. Nell Bane never claimed to have forged the memoir nor has Willoughby ever claimed that the writing was strictly his. Henry has brought copies of his memoir *My Place in the Gallery of Rogues* tonight and you may purchase a copy that Henry will be very pleased to sign."

Robert Hutchins and Edward Glendenning had set up an area in the atrium for book signing and Elizabeth Beaman had commissioned a handsome poster advertising the book. Now, assisted by Robert, Henry took his seat behind the table and guests began lining up to purchase copies.

"Are you pleased with yourself?" Bunty asked, drifting up to Nell's elbow. She held a small paper plate with a few desserts. "You should be. It's been quite a party."

CHAPTER 52

It was three weeks since the gala. Three weeks since Nell had heard from Henry Willoughby, so when she did hear, she felt her heart lighten with pleasure. Would Nell be home to company?

She was.

Henry came bundling into the house, bulky and awkward with parcels. She raised an inquiring eyebrow, but Henry simply set these down in a corner and seated himself on the sofa in the snug.

"You should have a hassock," he told her.

Nell smiled.

"Did you come all the way from Newbury to tell me that?"

"No, I came all the way from Newbury to read you a letter."

Assuming an air of importance, Henry took a letter from a breast pocket and with some ceremony, unfolded it. He glanced up at her.

"Walpole," he announced significantly.

Nell instantly braced herself against the old feeling.

Dear Willoughby,

Locked away as I am here in Walpole, I am nonetheless not locked away from the news. Most of it is revolting. I did read, however, of your triumph at the Pingree Cabot Museum. You turned the tables on them this time, boy-o, and good on ye. Had them toasting you in champagne apparently and eating out of your palm. Well, I'll be in here several seasons longer—thanks in part to your insistence on singing to the PCM about that Charlotte Amberson sketch—but I'll see you when I come out. You may be sure of that! We have some unfinished business to take care of.

As ever,
Stone

Henry folded the letter and tucked it away.

Nell was appalled.

"What does he mean by unfinished business? He's still threatening, isn't he? He's in the slammer and he still hasn't given up, the bully!"

"That chapter is ended." Henry seemed unflappable. "Now on to the next."

He rose and retrieved his bundles which he promptly unwrapped, revealing three small oil paintings of the salt marshes around the manse. The fourth was a watercolor of the manse itself—a wistful little portrait of an old New England farmhouse.

"I would like you to give these to Bunty and Ann. It is my hope that they will sell and make some money for the Backstreet Guild of Artists and Craftsmen. It is a good little shop and a noble cause. Heaven knows, gallery space for artists to display their talents is scarce, and I applaud our friends for their efforts to correct that."

"But you must give them the paintings yourself," Nell

protested.

Henry made brushing gestures.

"Haven't time," he said. "I have a flight booked to Paris and after that, I'm heading to the south of France to visit Muriel. I've been saying long enough how much I want to see her, and that sneaker slogan was the tipping point. 'Just do it', it says. So I am."

"Henry!" Nell was delighted. "But the manse? The Shop?"

"All tidied up and squared away," Henry declared. "They'll be fine until I return. If I decide to return, that is."

"So you have your tickets," Nell said. "Do you have your passport?"

"Right here," Henry produced it and wagged it at her.

"Is it... is it..." there was trepidation in Nell's voice.

"Is it legal?" Henry finished her sentence. An elfin bit of mischief played at the corners of his grin. "Well, what do you think? It'll get me past the TSA and on my way to France. I will write to you, my dear."

"Oh, Henry," Nell sighed, "we did have fun, didn't we?"

"It was," agreed H.H. Willoughby, "a swell trip!"

THE GHOST AND THE FORGER

Acknowledgements

This book began the evening my husband remarked he'd always wanted to be a forger. Actually, it began the evening I *heard* him say that. On that particular evening, the impact struck me and the next day I began writing *The Ghost and the Forger*. I am indebted to Don Doyle for the idea, for reading the manuscript and for the advice about Quinacridone Gold.

I am grateful to Robin Krolikowski for her sauerkraut soup recipe. Nell Bane may have tweaked it a bit, for which I hope she will be forgiven.

www.ingramcontent.com/pod-product-compliance
Lightning Source LLC
Chambersburg PA
CBHW031538260626

R18495600001B/R184956PG47155CBX00001B/1